AMERICAN D-BOY III

RISE OF THE DIAZ BROTHERS

BILLIGOAT

Paperback ISBN: 978-1-957954-91-2

eBook ISBN: 978-1-957954-92-9

This is a work of fiction. Names, characters, businesses, organizations, places, events, and incidents are either the product of the author's imagination or used in a fictitious manner. Any resemblance to actual persons, living or dead, or actual events is purely coincidental.

Published by Wahida Clark Presents Publishing

www.wclarkpublishing.com

Cover design by Nuance Art LLC | nuanceartllc.com

Printed in the United States of America

AMERICAN D-BOY III

RISE OF THE DIAZ BROTHERS

Written By BILLIGOAT

Wahida Clark's Innovative Publishin

CHAPTER 1
THE DIAZ BROTHERS

THE DIAZ BROTHERS' MANSION, SANDY SPRINGS, GEORGIA

Fernando and Diego quickly made their way to the top of the food chain in the drug business. Their brand of cocaine was called Super-Coke until YC did a song and called it "Nitro." The song quickly became number one in the country when the Diaz brothers' high-quality product started sweeping the nation. They couldn't keep up with the demand, which increased the price. One kilogram of Nitro went for $50,000.

When the Diaz brothers first manufactured their product back in Medellín, Colombia, they had no idea what they were doing. They were taking instructions from their Uncle Diaz, one of the top-ranking members of the Lost Souls Cartel. He was taught by the old-school farmers who kept their farming methods a secret.

Fernando recalled the day Uncle Diaz told them the key to growing potent products, and Diego laughed it off.

"I'm telling you that if you water your cocaine fields with cow urine, you'll produce coke that will have a psychedelic feeling to the hyperactive effect that coke gives you normally," Uncle Diaz said with a straight face while slightly swaying from drinking.

The brothers both laughed hysterically. "How are we going to get enough cow urine to water a field of coke?" Fernando asked while still laughing.

"All you need is a gallon, and you mix it in with a 50-gallon drum of water. And you only do it once for every crop. You will have the most potent cocaine in the world." Uncle Diaz was so convincing that Fernando turned serious.

"I'm going to do it; I'm going to find a way to get gallons of cow piss to water my crops." Fernando nodded his head and scratched his chin.

"You're not serious," Diego said. "You know Uncle Diaz is always telling us these crazy stories about the past."

"I'm telling you; it's a long-lost secret because it was too potent." Uncle Diaz took a swig straight from the bottle of the 100 percent proof tequila he was holding.

"Look at him. He's talking from that bottle. And you'll be a fool if you spray our crops with cow piss." Diego walked away toward the house. "I'm going to bed. I'll leave you two out here to talk about cow piss," he said, laughing to himself.

The next day, Fernando found a way to buy cow piss from a local farmer for $5.50 a gallon. Diego didn't have any idea that Fernando followed through with their uncle's advice . . . and it worked. At first, Fernando didn't know the effects of the cow piss until the customers started begging for the product it produced. It was the only coke they wanted.

One day, Diego noticed how the customers were feigning for the new crop they produced. "Is it me, or is this batch super potent? I've never seen people act like this from cocaine."

Fernando just smiled. "I did it," he shouted.

"You did what?" Diego asked curiously.

"I had the farmer spray our crops with cow piss, and it worked. We have the best cocaine in the world " Fernando was excited to know the positive results of his uncle's recipe.

"I can't believe you did it, and it worked. But I've never seen customers act like this," Diego responded.

"We have to keep this a secret. The only one who knows is you. The farmer doesn't even know what's in the jugs I give him to spray on the crops," Fernando said with conviction.

"It's our secret," Diego gave Fernando a handshake, "you crazy motherfucker."

The Diaz brothers didn't know if their coke had serious side effects or anything. What they later found out was that Nitro was highly addictive, ten times more than heroin and crack. If you did Nitro one time, you were most likely going to do it for the rest of your life because the withdrawal symptoms were deadly. The tolerance level of using Nitro increased at an abnormal rate. If you tried to wean yourself off Nitro, you felt like dying. There wasn't any drug like methadone that was used to wean an addict off heroin for Nitro addicts. You were effectively on a one-way ticket to being hooked for life.

It was the new drug of choice for Gen Z. After YC's hit song, "Nitro," caught fire, all the young rappers, bloggers, and influencers were using it and promoting it in their music and on their platforms. It was common to see the popular crowd doing Nitro while jamming to the song "Nitro" at ritzy parties. That's what catapulted the drug into the stratosphere in such a short time.

Fernando called a meeting to discuss the future of their empire. Sitting in attendance was "Mr. Nitro" himself, the young rap phenomenon YC, Carlos, Diego, and, of course, the boss man, Fernando. They had amassed 100 soldiers in the streets of Atlanta through YC. YC was the most popular rapper in the ATL, so he had the power to recruit. Carlos was a part of another cartel before jumping ship, so he also had connections in the city. The four-man team represented the hierarchy of what they called "The Diaz Cartel."

"This meeting is now in session," Fernando stated. "I want to inform you that we made $150 million in *six months*, and I estimate that we will make a quarter of a billion dollars in the next three months." Fernando spoke like a general to the round table of men.

"What will we do about King Cobra and the Lost Souls Cartel? He's threatening to raid our facilities. We need to exterminate him immediately," Diego spoke with vigor.

"I have a plan for him as well. After he killed our beloved Uncle Diaz, I recruited a small band of Lost Soul soldiers who are working undercover for us. Most of his top brass have turned on him. King Cobra just doesn't know it yet. His assassination will be any day now. It's just a matter of time," Fernando smiled.

"What about the plug to ship tons of Nitro to America?" Carlos asked. "We could make $100 million monthly if we could get more than 1,000 kilos shipped at a time."

"I'm on it," YC chimed in. "I pressed Haitian John about it, but he isn't telling me anything. However, I know he knows a way to get more shipped."

"Maybe we need to persuade him. Tell him I got $500K for his information," Fernando proposed.

"I got you; I'm supposed to meet with him and G-Mack later today," YC replied.

"Oh yeah. What's the deal with that dude, whatshis-name D-Boy?" Fernando asked YC.

"I asked Haitian John about that situation. He isn't telling me anything other than, 'He's somebody I know from back in the day in New York.' That's all he has to say," YC responded.

"If you can contact D-Boy to get more information about his connection with Haitian John, it might be fruitful. Something isn't adding up the way you said Haitian John acted like he saw a ghost." Fernando remembered what YC told him.

"I know, that shit was crazy. I just know there's more to it than what Haitian John is telling me. But he keeps in contact because he needs me to move his coke, which I stopped moving because of Nitro. No one wants his shit. It's weak compared to Nitro," YC explained.

"Pedro is on his way back with 1,000 kilos, which will be gone in a week. We need a connection to ship tons. Then we can make several billion a year, maybe more. There's no competition," Diego said.

"G-Mack has D-Boy's contact, and he's also acting funny about the situation. G-Mack introduced me to Haitian John, so they both been acting weird about that whole shit that went down that day." YC recalled how G-Mack and Haitian John were both standoffish about the topic.

"You're right. See what you can find out about D-Boy and the connect to ship in more work," Diego added.

"Hopefully, YC can get it out of Haitian John. It's riskier doing these small trips. We have so many orders for bricks of Nitro that we could move a ton in about a month, tops," Carlos said.

YC looked at his iced-out Patek Phillipe watch. "Fuck! I'm supposed to be at Nobu in half an hour to meet with G-Mack and Haitian John. I forgot G-Mack moved the time up because he has a flight to catch. I'll let you know what I find out." He stood up, raced out of the mansion to his jet-black Rolls-Royce Wraith, and sped away.

NOBU RESTAURANT, BUCKHEAD, ATLANTA

The patrons of Nobu were always of the prestigious stock of the Buckhead section of Atlanta. Everything was priced to ensure that no one who wasn't making at least six figures would want to eat there. The décor was always extravagant, which added to the rich ambiance.

G-Mack and Haitian John sat in the back in a corner

booth, waiting for YC to arrive. "This guy can't be on time to save his life," G-Mack complained.

"Agent Heron instructed me to debrief him on any questions pertaining to D-Boy," Haitian John said nervously.

"What's with this guy D-Boy? What's the big secret about him that you and Agent Heron are keeping?" G-Mack asked.

You could tell someone important had just entered Nobu because everyone began to whisper, "Is that YC?"

"I'm here with a party of two." YC looked around and saw G-Mack and John in the corner. "I see my people over there." He strolled in the direction of his party.

"I fuck with that 'Nitro' song. That's all I play in my whip," the waiter said excitedly. "Can I take a pic with you?" He pulled out his phone and was ready to take the photo.

"Sure." YC took a quick picture with the eager fan.

"Thank you, YC." The fan put his phone in his pocket and escorted YC to his table.

Haitian John was about to speak when YC was ushered to the table. "Pardon me for the lateness. I had a meeting prior to this one that was an hour from here," YC explained.

"It's cool as long as you made it," G-Mack replied. "Now, let's get down to business."

"Let's do it." YC was ready to hear whatever business he had on the table.

Haitian John spoke first. "We had an agreement. You were supposed to move the work for me. What happened?"

"I'll be honest. Your work is trash compared to Nitro. That shit sells more than crack in the '80s," YC explained.

"You know where to get it?" G-Mack asked.

"Do I! I'm plugged in directly with the Diaz brothers," YC said.

"Who are the Diaz brothers?" Haitian John asked.

"The Diaz brothers are the ones who created the Nitro. They were members of the Lost Souls Cartel from Medellín, Colombia," YC answered.

Haitian John looked at G-Mack before speaking. "You can get kilos of it?"

"That's what I wanted to talk to you about. They need a better way to transport Nitro to the United States. I know you have the plug that he needs. Fernando is offering $500K for the plug to safely transport a couple of tons of Nitro to the United States." YC made the offer that Fernando put on the table.

"I would have to get back to you on that. You're talking about a big connection; this isn't some small task," Haitian John explained.

"I know, but there's a lot of money in shipping Nitro. I'm talking about *billions*," YC replied.

"I'll have an answer for you by the end of the day," Haitian John said.

"That's fair." YC paused. "What's the deal with the dude you called D-Boy?"

Haitian John looked at G-Mack before speaking. "He's an old enemy I had from back in the day in New York. He's nothing for you to worry about. Do you have contact with him?" Haitian John asked nervously.

"I don't, but what if I did? What's it to you? Why the

secrecy around this dude? I know what you told me, but I feel like there's more to it," YC spoke conspicuously.

"I know it looks like something serious. Let's just say I thought he was taken care of. So, when I saw him, I was surprised, that's all. No more, no less," Haitian John explained.

"OK. Just let me know if you can get that shipping connect, and you'll have that $500K wired to your account," YC said before standing up to leave.

"You never told me if you're going to sell my work. That was our agreement," Haitian John replied, trying to get YC back on his team.

"I told you, no one wants your work once they get Nitro. I got the connect if you want that Nitro." YC smiled before exiting Nobu.

When YC left the restaurant, Agent Heron calmly strolled to their table and sat down. Haitian John and G-Mack looked at each other, then at Agent Heron. They didn't know he was present at their meeting. They also didn't realize he had a microphone hidden at their table, so he heard the entire conversation.

"That was interesting . . . Nitro. I've been hearing whispers about it," Agent Heron said smugly.

How the fuck did he know what we were talking about? G-Mack thought to himself before responding. "Me too. That's all my customers keep asking for."

"I'm not going to front; I heard about Nitro too. But until today, I didn't know where to get it," Haitian John added.

"I want you to tell YC you're taking him up on his offer." Agent Heron paused to send Haitian John a text message. "This is my private contact and bank account number I want the $500K sent to."

Haitian John looked disappointed. "I'm just saying, can't I get at least $50K for being the middleman?"

"Be thankful for the money we're paying you. Anything extra belongs to the Agency." Agent Heron stood up. "Good day, gentlemen." Then he exited the building.

"Did you know he was here?" G-Mack asked.

"I had no idea, and how did he hear the conversation about the shipping connect?" Haitian John asked.

"Good question. Our phones must be tapped for listening. You know the CIA has access to all that technology," G-Mack replied.

"You're right. There's no escaping these motherfuckers," Haitian John said before gulping down his Long Island Iced Tea.

"If I were you, I would send that text over to YC ASAP. You know how Heron can get. You don't want to piss him off, if you know what I mean." G-Mack spoke with concern.

"You're right. I'm about to send it to him now." Haitian John took out his phone and forwarded the message to YC. Then he called him.

"What up? You got good news for me?" YC asked.

"Check your text message," Haitian John said.

YC looked at the message and smiled. "*That's* what's up! I'm going to get at the Diaz brothers immediately with this info. Good looking, my nigga."

YC hung up and called Fernando. "Yo, I got it. I'm about to text you the info."

"You got the shipping connect?" Fernando asked with excitement.

"Facts, my nigga. I'm sending the text now," YC said.

Fernando looked at the phone. "I got it." He paused, "Did you find out anything about this D-Boy character?"

"I asked again, but Haitian John gave me the same generic answer. He said D-Boy was someone he had beef with back in New York. That was all he said about him."

"I can't put my finger on it, but I feel like D-Boy can be an important asset to our organization," Fernando said mysteriously.

"Whatever I can find out, I'll let you know. Other than that, I did my part. I got the shipping connect; now, let's get to it," YC said.

"I got you, brother. This is the start of the biggest drug empire in history," Fernando said with vigor.

"Let's get it, bro," YC replied with equal energy.

CHAPTER 2
LOWER EAST SIDE OF MANHATTAN, ALPHABET CITY

D-Boy was still getting used to being back in the States. He had to watch his back carefully because the threat of Agent Heron was still looming. The only good thing was that Heron didn't have the backing of the CIA. If he did, D-Boy and John would be "erased," as the Agency likes to call it. They didn't like to leave any loose ends.

John knew how to strategize around the fact that this was a rogue operation run by Agent Heron and a few willing participating agents. It wasn't uncommon for senior agents to partake in extracurricular activities that the director didn't sanction. History shows many accounts of agents lining their pockets with money from these types of operations. Most see it as a perk of being in the Agency.

"From my calculations, Agent Heron doesn't want anyone to know we're alive. It would raise questions at the Agency, which would cause problems Heron doesn't want. We are safe for now, but that doesn't mean that Heron didn't assemble a team of rogue agents to work with him," John said like a master tactician.

"What about the Feds?" D-Boy asked.

"They most likely closed the case after seven years. That's their policy for cold cases, so we're good on that front," John responded.

"It sounds like we're good. I'm tired of living in the shadows. I know I can't be on social media making posts, but I just want to live a normal life," D-Boy added.

"Our lives will never be normal, so just accept that. We will *always* have to look behind our backs. That is, until the threat is eliminated," John said.

"I assume the threat is Agent Heron."

"Right. If we take out Heron, all our problems are solved." John squinted his eyes.

"So, let's take this motherfucker out," D-Boy said.

"If it were only that easy, but that is the plan. Take out Agent Heron and the girl Sarah."

"I almost forgot about Sarah. I know Dirty Redd is fucked up behind her—" D-Boy was interrupted by a knock on the door.

John pulled out his weapon before moving toward the door and looking through the peephole. "Speak of the devil; it's Jay-Roc and Dirty Redd." John opened the door and looked down the hall to ensure no one was tailing them.

Jay-Roc and Dirty Redd entered the apartment and gave D-Boy and John handshakes before sitting on the sofa. Dirty Redd had a sad expression on his face that told the story of a heartbroken man. He fell fast and hard for Sarah, known as Agent Sparrow to the CIA. He tried his best to hide his emotions but wore them on his sleeve. Every man knew what Dirty Redd was going through, but it was heart wrenching watching someone suffer.

"Cheer up, my man," D-Boy said while tapping Dirty Redd on his back. "If it was meant to be, it would be. Everything happens for a reason, right, John?" D-Boy recalled the lesson while looking at John for confirmation.

"That's absolutely right, my friend. The reason is always connected to a purpose. You'll figure out the purpose in due time," John spoke like a guru of truth.

"Plus, women outnumber men seven to one, and in places like Atlanta, it's something like 15 to one," D-Boy exclaimed excitedly.

Dirty Redd nodded in agreement. "You're right. I heard the ratio of men to women is crazy in Atlanta because they have so many gay guys, leaving all the baddies for straight men."

"That's the spirit." D-Boy tapped him on his back again.

Jay-Roc interrupted. "I don't mean to break up your little male-bonding session, but I came here to tell you that Grandpa Joe had a stroke, and he's in the hospital."

D-Boy instantly got serious. "Is he OK?"

"We don't know yet. This is his second stroke since you been gone. The doctor said he's too old for surgery, so there's nothing they can do but give him medication and wait it out," Jay-Roc responded.

"Fuck those medications! I follow this dude named Yahki Awakened, who is teaching people natural remedies to everything," D-Boy said confidently.

"His doctor did say there's one thing they may help him, and that's if he goes on a strict vegan/plant-based diet.

He said he's recommending that more ofter. these days because the evidence is overwhelming that it actually works."

"You know Grandpa Joe ain't going on nc plant-based vegan anything. He was raised in the South on pigs, chickens, and cows. Trying to get him to give that up will be impossible," D-Boy stated before continuing. "But it's still worth a try. We can make things for him and not tell him they're plant-based. When I was in Dubai, I ate falafels, which are fried chickpeas, for a year without knowing it. And it was delicious."

"Me and Pops was talking about that; he said the same thing," Jay-Roc responded.

"Man, Pops," D-Boy paused. "I miss the hell out of him and Grandpa Joe. If it wasn't for you, I wouldn't have no connection with my family."

Grandpa Joe and D-Boy's father, OG Jesse, had no idea that D-Boy faked his death. They believed that his body was blown to bits in that Mercedes-Benz seven years ago. Jay-Roc was the only person who knew besides D-Boy and John, and Jay-Roc found out by mistake. Jay-Roc stumbled upon the truth when he followed John to the safe house, where he was made privy to the plot of the fake deaths. Other than that, John made sure this operation was ironclad.

Jay-Roc discovering the fake deaths turned out to be a great move on the chessboard for John and D-Boy. Jay-Roc ran American D-Boy records and apparel up to the sum of $250 million in seven years. He could wire almost $50 million in increments to them as a cushion for their stay in the luxuriously extravagant Dubai.

"What hospital is he in? I want to visit him," D-Boy asked.

"He's at Jamaica Hospital," Jay-Roc answered.

When D-Boy asked Jay-Roc what hospital Grandpa Joe was in, John immediately began to tweak opening and closing his eyes. He was having a moment of total recall from his days as an Israeli Intelligence Agent for Mossad. He remembered an operation where he had to target a family member to lure his prey into a trap:

"How are you today?" John asked while smiling at the old lady sitting on the park bench as he sat beside her.

"I'm doing good. Thanks for asking," she responded.

John gently touched the lady's hands. "God bless your soul! I wish I live to be your age." He smiled and looked into her eyes.

"Thank you so much. I can tell you—" Before she could finish her sentence, the potent neurotoxin set in, and she closed her eyes. Her body slumped onto John's shoulder.

John removed the fingertip injection pads before a black van pulled up, and a sliding door opened. A tall, muscular guy got out, swiftly picked up the old lady, and tossed her into the van. Once inside the vehicle, John pulled out his cell phone and made a FaceTime call. When the recipient answered, John had the camera facing the old lady, knocked out in a seat.

"We got your nana, so if you ever want to see her again, meet me at these coordinates." He then hung up.

D-Boy noticed John's behavior. He's seen him do this before. "John, what's happening?"

John snapped out of his daydream. "We have to get to Jamaica Hospital ASAP." He jumped up and quickly headed for the door, but no one moved. "Let's go! Unless you don't want to see your grandfather again."

Everyone moved in unison with John's order. They all headed for the blacked-out Suburban John liked to drive. The inside was like a mobile command center equipped with surveillance cameras, night vision, smoke screen, and 50-caliber gun turrets around the vehicle. It also had four drones that would deploy from hidden compartments in the roof. Computer screens lined the dashboard, giving a 360-degree panoramic view around the vehicle. It had an 800-hp V12 engine, making it the fastest Suburban on the street. Last but not least, it was entirely bulletproof. D-Boy called it a tank; John called it the Warlord because of its destructive ability.

When they got to the garage, the Warlord was already growling and ready to go. Jay-Roc was impressed with the mean-looking Suburban. He remembered the day seven years ago when John posed as the bum at D-Boy's funeral. He wondered if this was the same truck John dipped off to D-Boy's stash spot in Long Island.

"This shit is tough. What is this, some kind of military vehicle?" Dirty Redd asked in amazement.

"It's something like that," John replied.

"Is this the same truck you had seven years ago when I followed you to Long Island?" Jay-Roc asked curiously.

"You have a good memory. It is the same truck."

Jay-Roc noticed all of the screens showing him the rear of the truck. he thought back to that day when he followed John. *He had all these cameras, so he knew I was following him that day.*

"John, let me ask you a question," Jay-Roc said.

"Sure." John liked questions.

"That day I followed you back to Long Island, you knew I was following you because the cameras in this truck let you see everything, right?"

John smiled. "You got me. Luring you back to the headquarters in Long Island was my plan."

"All this time, I thought Jay-Roc just got lucky when he found us that day." D-Boy had a revelation.

"I couldn't tell you everything. You know the old saying, never let your left hand know what your right hand is doing. Jay-Roc had to be tested before I was sure that we could let him in on our plans. I also knew that we needed someone in the States working with us, so what better person than Jay-Roc?" John was trained to be the master of unpredictability. "Remember, we have to stay not one but—"

"Seven moves ahead of our opponent." D-Boy finished John's sentence because he drilled that into him for the last seven years.

JAMAICA HOSPITAL, JAMAICA QUEENS, NYC

Grandpa Joe was lying in the comfortable hospital bed, flipping through the channels with the remote control in his hand. "I don't wanna watch none of this shit. What happened to the days when you could watch a program without seeing men kissing?" he aggressively changed the channel to an old western. "Now, this is more like it. Something I can relate to."

As he was watching his show, a tall, muscular man dressed in a nurse outfit pushing a wheelchair entered the room. "How are you doing today, Mr. Jensen? I'm here to take you to get an MRI," he said with a hint of some foreign accent.

Grandpa Joe sat up straight. "Oh no, the fuck you are not! And who the fuck are you? Where is my regular doctor? I don't fuck with none of you foreigners since . . . hell, since never! Now get the fuck up—" Before Grandpa Joe could finish his sentence, the man quickly jabbed him in the arm with a powerful substance that rendered him unconscious immediately. He picked up Grandpa Joe's limp body as if it were a ragdoll and tossed it into the wheelchair.

"I have the asset. Be ready for extraction," he said through the AirPod planted in his ear.

"I'm here parked as planned," the female voice on the other side responded.

The man pushed Grandpa Joe's limp body toward the elevator. Then he got a message from the female voice. "We have company."

THE TITANIUM black Suburban pulled up into the garage, and D-Boy, John, Jay-Roc, and Dirty Redd jumped out, ran toward the right, and pressed the button for the elevator to come down. As they were waiting, John scanned the garage for anything suspicious.

He didn't recognize the blacked-out minivan sitting to their left, but she saw them and immediately used the laptop to show her the cameras on the elevator and the eighth floor where Grandpa Joe's room was located.

"This has to be the slowest elevator in Queens," D-Boy shouted.

They all watched as the numbers above the elevator showed what floor it was on. It came down from the fifteenth floor and stopped on the eighth floor. They watched as it stopped on that floor.

"That's Grandpa Joe's floor the elevator is stopping on," Jay-Roc announced as they all watched the elevator.

SHE SAW the four men running toward the elevator. She knew them all, but one was her old assignment. She became very intimate with him, to where she caught feelings for him. That violated rule number one: Never get emotionally attached to your assignment. It could ruin the whole operation.

"You still look good." She felt butterflies in her stomach. She wanted to take a knife and cut them out. She resented the way she was feeling about Dirty Redd, especially when she was carrying his baby.

"Don't get on the elevator yet. His family just arrived. Push him to the hallway left of the elevator and wait for my signal," the female said.

"OK, let me know." He made a left, pushed the wheelchair in front of a water fountain, and began drinking until she gave him the green light to go.

The elevator opened, three nurses exited the eighth floor, and one person got on. The elevator was headed straight for the parking garage. The two people got out and headed toward their cars when it got to the garage. The lady noticed the urgency of the four men getting onto the elevator.

"Have a nice day, miss," John said, sensing her energy shift when they bombarded the elevator like the Feds.

"You too," she replied with a smile before the automatic doors shut in her face.

No one spoke as the elevator rode to the eighth floor. When it stopped and opened, they all followed Jay-Roc because he was the only one who knew what room Grandpa Joe was in. They headed straight for the front desk to check in.

"We're here to see Joeseph Jenkins in room 805," Jay-Roc said.

"Sure," the attendant responded.

Then they dashed in the direction of his room.

"Now!" she shouted into his ear.

He quickly pushed the wheelchair to the elevator and waited for it to open. While he stood there, a cute redheaded nurse came beside him and was waiting for the elevator too.

"That's Mr. Jenkins from room 805. He is so frisky for an old man. The other day he palmed my ass." She smiled.

"I hear the Black guys last until their dying day," he smiled back.

She batted her eyes. "Where is he going?"

He hesitated, and the elevator bell rang. The doors opened. "Oh, I'm taking him to the MRI room. Maybe you can take my number, and we can hang out sometime." She forgot all about her question and took her cell phone from her pocket.

"HE'S NOT IN HERE!" Jay-Roc shouted. "He wasn't scheduled to be taken out of his room for anything."

John looked around the room and noticed that his chart was still on the bed, which indicated that he was abruptly taken.

"Let's go!" John moved back toward the elevator.

As he turned the corner, the elevator doors were closing, but not before he saw Grandpa Joe slumped in the wheelchair and the face of a man he remembered from his years as an agent in Mossad.

"It can't be," he said to himself before the man smiled and the doors closed.

D-Boy noticed the look on John's face. "What happened? Did you see something?"

"They got Grandpa Joe," John said solemnly.

"Who the fuck is 'they'?" D-Boy asked.

"I'm not sure yet, but my best guess is Agent Heron." John withheld the information about the glimpse of the man from his past.

"What do we do now?" Jay-Roc asked.

"We wait for the call with instructions on how to get him back," John responded while walking toward the elevator.

They all followed suit and got on the elevator, then dashed to the Suburban. As soon as they got in, John made verbal commands to the car's computer. "Warlord, hack into Jamaica Hospital's video feed from 15 minutes ago from the eighth floor and the elevator."

The screens on the dashboard showed the eighth floor by the elevator, showing doctors and nurses walking around, tending to patients. Then they saw a tall, muscular man with dark hair pushing a wheelchair. As they got closer, they recognized the person in the wheelchair as Grandpa Joe. The dark-haired man headed straight for the elevator but then made a quick detour and stopped at the water fountain. Then they saw the elevator doors open, and D-Boy, Jay-Roc, Dirty Redd, and John exited the elevator toward the room. That's when the guy pushed the wheelchair to the elevator and spoke to the nurse as he waited to get on the elevator. When it stopped in the garage, a black minivan pulled up, and a female was seen opening the side door.

"Warlord, freeze the frame and zoom in on the female."

When it zoomed in, Dirty Redd took a deep breath, and his heart skipped a beat. "That's Sarah!" he shouted.

"Which lets me know that this is the work of Agent Heron. He's recruited another rogue agent to work for him," John said.

"Fuck all that. How do we get Grandpa Joe back?" D-Boy demanded.

"We get him back by playing chess with our opponent. They made the first move. What happens after this is up to us because it's our move. This is real life, so we have to relax and strategically think about our next move. It could mean life or death."

CHAPTER 3
SAFE HOUSE IN MARIETTA, GEORGIA

AGENT HERON SAT behind a desk looking at a laptop when he saw the black minivan pull into the garage. He stood up and walked through the side door to the garage to greet Agent J and Sarah. Grandpa Joe was just coming out of his slumber when J put him into the wheelchair.

"Where the hell am I?" Grandpa Joe asked groggily from the effects of the drug. He tried to focus on the face before him, and then it came to him. "You're the mother-fucker that stuck me with that needle."

"That I am, and if you don't shut the fuck up, I'm going to stick something else in you that you're not going to like. You understand me?" Agent J said with the undertone of a sadistic torturer.

Grandpa Joe knew when to play it cool. "Hey, look, man, I don't know what this is about, but I'm sure my grandson Jay-Roc can pay you whatever."

Agent J didn't respond. He just pushed his chair toward Heron, who was waiting in the foyer.

"Grandpa Joe, it's a pleasure to meet you finally. I studied your family tree a lot, and it's quite interesting. Your family has been hustling since slavery." He stuck his hand out to get a handshake, but Grandpa Joe didn't shake it.

"I don't shake hands with snakes," Grandpa Joe said with venom.

"That's fine, but you mentioned your grandson Jay-Roc. Would you happen to have his number so we can leave him a message?" Heron asked.

"That depends. What's in it for me?" Joe asked.

"For starters, you get to keep breathing, or I could let Agent J force it out of you."

Agent J grinned. "I have some new torture techniques I would love to test on him."

Grandpa Joe got serious. He knew this was no time for his antics. He knew when to throw in his hand. His expression went from defiant to defeated. He knew he was in over his head this time. Not even all the game in the world would get him out of this one. All he could think about was what this could really be about.

"OK, but before I give you his number, could you at least tell me what this is all about? I'm an old man in his last days, so it doesn't matter, but I'm not putting my grandson's life in jeopardy."

Agent Heron nodded. "I understand, so I'm going to let you in on a little secret since you mentioned you didn't want to put your grandson's life in danger." He paused to find the right way to say it. "What if I told you that you're not just putting one of your grandson's lives in danger, but *both* of your grandsons' lives on the line?"

Grandpa Joe squinted his eyes and cocked his head to the side. "Wait a minute, I only have *one* living grandson. D-Boy died seven years ago."

Agent Heron looked at Sarah, who was just joining the party. "Did I miss anything?"

"Not at all. You're just in time for the moment of truth, the great reveal."

Grandpa Joe was confused. "What the fuck are you talking about, man? Just be straight up. Enough of this ring-around-the-rosy bullshit."

"I like that. So, what if I told you that the one and only Darius 'D-Boy' Jensen is alive and well?" Agent Heron watched his facial expression show disbelief.

Grandpa Joe laughed. "D-Boy died seven years ago in a car bombing. He was blown to smithereens."

"That's what he *wanted* the world to believe, but the truth is that he faked his death. He is very much alive. And you will give me Jay-Roc's number to save all of your lives."

Grandpa Joe shook his head. "I lived a long and prosperous life. I did some bad things that I regret, but I've never been a snitch or a chump. But here . . ."

Agent Heron took out his phone and dialed the number. It rang twice before someone answered.

"Hello, who is this?"

Agent Heron requested to FaceTime, and the screen showed Jay-Roc's face. Heron turned the phone's screen around to show Grandpa Joe sitting in the wheelchair.

"Grandpa Joe! You OK? They didn't hurt you, did they?" Jay-Roc said, breathless.

"I'm good. They tried to make me give you up. I told them I'm no chump. Do what you got to do."

"He's a tough cookie." Agent Heron showed his smiling face.

"Heron!" D-Boy grabbed the phone from Jay-Roc's hand. "If you touch one hair on his body, I'm going to kill you."

"Well, well, the star of the show. How you been? It's been awhile, like seven years, to be exact."

Grandpa Joe couldn't believe what he was hearing. "D-Boy! Is that *really* you?" Tears welled up in his eyes.

"Yeah, it's me, Grandpa Joe. I'm going to get you out of this mess, I promise you," D-Boy professed.

"I'll be calling you back with instructions." Agent Heron hung up the phone. "See, that wasn't so bad. I just wanted to test you, and I must say you are as tough as they come. Take him to his room and make sure it's secure. We wouldn't want him escaping."

"I was looking forward to twisting the information out of him," Agent J said before wheeling him to the secured room and locking the door.

"Now, it's time for phase two of my plan." Agent Heron made another call. "What's popping, my G?" he said in a mock urban accent.

"Another day, another dollar," Haitian John answered.

"Good news. I will introduce you to the plug for shipping tons of Nitro. Meet me by the Mercedes-Benz Stadium in half an hour."

"Copy." Haitian John picked up his car keys and headed to the destination.

Agent Heron looked at Agent J. "You ready?"

"Of course, is that a trick question?" he responded.

They headed to the stadium, leaving Sarah at the safe house. When they arrived, they saw Haitian John sitting in his car. They pulled up beside him, got out, then climbed into John's car. Heron sat in the front seat, and Agent J sat in the back behind Heron.

"John, this is Jarvis. He's the owner of one of the largest shipping companies in the world," Heron announced.

"Nice to meet you, Jarvis." Haitian John extended his hand, and Agent J shook it very firmly. "You got a strong grip, my guy."

Agent J just smiled while staring at John with a menacing grin because he knew the toxins were starting to kick in. On the tips of his fingers were microneedles that didn't puncture but were small enough to inject lethal toxins into the microscopic pores in the epidermis. The recipient didn't feel a thing, making it so effective.

"What the fuck?" Haitian John tried to move his head. "I can't move." All the movements of his body were paralyzed.

"Sorry, John. The Agency doesn't like loose ends. Besides, the Haitian mob paid me good money for your execution," Heron said as he and Agent J got out. "You have the instructions on how they want him done?"

"I added a treat in it for me. I gave him just the right amount so he would feel everything," Agent J responded with sadistic glee.

"Have fun. I'll see you back at the safe house." Heron got into his car and drove off.

Agent J got in the front seat. "This is going to be so much fun. I'm excited."

He took his hands and grabbed John's face as if to embrace it. Then he pressed his thumbs into his eye sockets with so much force that his eyeballs instantly popped into his hands. "See no evil."

John screamed out in pain.

Agent J took out a Ginsu pocketknife and sliced off John's right ear. "Hear no evil." Then he took one hand, opened John's mouth, pulled out his tongue, and cut it out. "Speak no evil."

By that time, John had passed out from the excruciating pain, but he was still alive. Not for long, though, as the blood gushed from his wounds. Agent J left the eyeballs, the ear, and the tongue on John's lap.

Agent J exited the car, ran his hand through his hair, and took a deep breath. He started to stroll away from the car, reveling in his actions. Agent J was one of the most inhuman torturers that Mossad had ever produced. Now, he was working with the CIA as a cleanup guy, although he left a bloody mess.

Agent J, whose real name was Johan Bernstein, was born and raised in Tel Aviv, Israel. His parents were super-successful jewelers who owned an illegal diamond mine in the Congo. They were partners with a brutal regime that practiced inhumane torture on the local villagers by chopping off their children's limbs for not reaching the designated quota. The international community has called for anyone associated with these illegal diamond mines to face charges of crimes against humanity. Despite the threat of a life sentence in prison, Johan's father continued his nefarious business dealings.

Johan didn't want to follow in the family's footsteps the traditional way. However, in an uncanny way, he took on a part of the family business. Johan loved the violence and torture that he cultivated from his days in the Israeli Defense Force. He just wanted to torture and kill. He was content not being a wealthy jeweler as long as he could feed his sadistic behavior with impunity.

Johan's first experience with torture was at the tender age of 18. He was on a search-and-destroy mission in the West Bank of Palestine. His platoon was ambushed by gunfire coming from an apartment complex. Johan took out a rocket launcher and aimed it at the area of the building that the gunfire was coming from. He hit the target dead center, causing the combatants to stop shooting.

As Johan's platoon got closer, they saw five combatants running from the building. Johan wanted them alive, so he aimed for their legs. Three of them fell, and the other two got away.

"Good job, Johan!" Sergeant Stein said. "You single-handedly neutralized the enemy, and now we have these three to interrogate."

The three men were lying on the ground, wincing from their leg wounds, when Johan walked over and stood over them. "Can I interrogate them since I'm the one that took them out?" he asked.

Sergeant Stein looked at the eagerness in Johan's eyes. "I'll let you torture them if they don't answer my questions."

"Torture them?" Johan thought about torturing his enemies. "I would love to torture these Palestinian dogs!"

"You men, get these dogs up, tie their hands behind their backs, and throw them in the truck," Sergeant Stein commanded.

They drove to an IDF substation right outside of the West Bank and took the detainees to a room with chairs that had leg shackles attached to them. They bound the prisoners' ankles to the legs of the chairs. The men were trying to be brave, but they knew what happened to captives of the IDF. Torture was an understatement; it was a slow, agonizing death.

"Leave Johan and me with the prisoners," Sergeant Stein ordered. The other men exited the room.

"I'm going to ask you some questions. If you decide to answer, I'll leave you alive. If not . . . Well, let's just say my friend Johan is eager to have his first experiment in the fine art of torture."

Johan was tall and lanky then, but he would fill out into a muscular giant. However, at that moment, he wasn't the menacing tower he is now, so the men almost laughed at the thought of this scrawny teenager torturing them.

Johan noticed the smirk on one of their faces, so he took the butt of his gun and smashed it into the man's left temple. "It's not so funny now, is it?"

The man's head began to bleed. "Easy, Killer! The object is to make them feel just the right amount of pain without killing them or rendering them unconscious like you just did. The art of interrogation is finding pressure points." Sergeant Stein stood in front of the second pris-

oner. Then he reached down and grabbed the prisoner's testicles and squeezed them.

"Owwwww!" the prisoner screamed.

"See, this is very painful, but it won't kill him. We need them alive and conscious so they can accurately answer questions." He paused. "For that, you need special tools." He took a pair of needle-nose pliers from his pocket. "I keep these in my pocket for times like this." Then he looked at the prisoner who had screamed. "Now, tell me where the Hamas headquarters in the West Bank is?" Then he clamped the pliers onto his right ear and pressed down.

"Owwwww! I'll tell you! Please, stop!"

"This one was easy. Sometimes, I must spend hours trying to break these Palestinian dogs."

"Let me try," Johan asked.

"There's nothing left to do. He's going to give us the information. They will all be taken to the holding cell to be processed."

"Let me practice on one of them," Johan said eagerly.

Sergeant Stein looked around. "I'll let you practice on this one. He's almost dead anyway. Just say he died from the bullet wounds." Sergeant Stein took the other two men with him. "Have fun," he said before exiting the room with his prisoners.

Johan grabbed the pliers that the sergeant had left him. He imagined all the ways he could torture this man without killing him. He took them and started clamping them down on all his fingers, then his toes. The man screamed in agony, but to no avail because the room was soundproof.

Then he took the pliers and jammed them in both of his ears until the man was deaf. Next, he used the tool to *remove his teeth and even squeezed the man's lips. He stuck the pliers up his nose, then clamped on the man's nipples until they ripped off.*

"Just kill me!" the prisoner screamed.

"Not yet. I'm beginning to understand what the sergeant was trying to teach me."

He continued torturing the man for the next three hours until the man died.

As Johan thought back to that day, his penis became erected. "Ah, the good old days."

His Uber pulled up beside him, so he got in and sat silently in the back as if he were a normal man. However, he was far from normal; Johan was a serial sadist with an appetite for killing. Agent Heron knew what type of man he recruited when he looked at his résumé. Johan was Hannibal Lector on steroids, with a license to kill.

When Agent J got to the safe house, Agent Heron and Sarah were sitting in the living room talking. They abruptly stopped speaking as if they didn't want Johan to hear their conversation. They didn't want him to know that they were lovers. Johan already thought they were an item based on how they looked at each other when they thought he wasn't paying attention.

"Did you have fun?" Heron asked sarcastically.

"It was therapeutic. I needed that."

"Now, we're ready to call D-Boy with instructions." Heron pulled out his phone and called the contact number for D-Boy. He picked up on the second ring. "My nigga, D-Boy. I really liked you. You were the best decoy I've had the opportunity to work with."

"I can't say the same. What do you want me to do to get my grandfather back?" D-Boy got straight to the point.

"Pack your bags. You're going to ATL, shorty," Heron mocked an Atlanta accent.

"Going to Atlanta to do what?"

"When you land, I'll be there to pick you up and give you further instructions. Your flight leaves at 8:00 a.m. tomorrow under the name Derrick Jenkins. I got it close to your government name, Darius Jensen," Heron informed him.

"What guarantee do I have that Grandpa Joe is healthy and alive?" D-Boy asked.

"Oh, you'll know he's alive because you'll see him often. When I'm done with you, you both can leave. Let's just say this is payback for outsmarting me, taking my drug money, and becoming a successful entrepreneur."

"That's typical of a devil. Mad because the righteous want to prevail. When I met you, I was 15 years old. I'm 30 now. I learned the most powerful lesson in life from you," D-Boy said.

"What lesson was that, D-Boy?"

"Never trust a snake." D-Boy hung up and looked at Jay-Roc and John.

CHAPTER 4
HARTSVILLE-JACKSON ATLANTA INTERNATIONAL AIRPORT

ATLANTA INTERNATIONAL AIRPORT is the busiest airport in America. It was always packed to the brim with flyers from around the world. When D-Boy landed, he remembered how busy it had been since he visited a year ago. He developed an affinity for Atlanta because of the historic Black excellence it represented. Atlanta has more Black-owned businesses per capita than anywhere in America.

D-Boy walked out to the arrival gate, looking for Agent Heron. A black Mercedes-Benz pulled up as he stood there, and the back window rolled down. "My nigga, D-Boy, welcome to the A, my boy!" Agent Heron couldn't waste an opportunity to mock Black culture.

"You know imitation is the highest form of flattery. In my hood, we call it 'Dick Riding,' no homo," D-Boy said nonchalantly while coldly staring Agent Heron in his eyes.

Agent Heron turned beet red because he didn't have a snappy comeback like usual. "Get in the fucking car," he said, showing a chink in his armor.

The trunk automatically opened, so D-Boy threw his luggage inside, closed it, and got in the backseat beside Agent Heron. He looked at the man for three seconds, then turned his head toward the window. The energy was intense but cordial. Each man had an agenda but on opposite sides of the coin.

D-Boy wanted to be left alone to live his life free from the clutches of his past and the CIA. He was a teen when Agent Heron approached him with an offer he knew D-Boy couldn't refuse. D-Boy and Jay-Roc were trying to survive the best way they knew how. Agent Heron knew about their story from the grapevine of criminal networks. He purposely chose them to groom them into the largest heroin dealers on the East Coast to make himself wealthy.

Agent Heron was doing this out of ego and a deep innate hatred for African Americans that stemmed from his upbringing in Jackson, Mississippi. He was raised by the Ku Klux Klan; his father and grandfather were both Grand Wizards. Michael, which was Agent Heron's real name, chose to lynch Blacks by poisoning their communities with tons of heroin. He knew the effects of dumping heroin in the Black community, and he also knew how much money there was in doing so.

"For me, smuggling heroin into the Black community is like killing two niggers with one stone. I'm lining my pockets and killing them off at the same time. My grand pappy would be proud of me," he once said to a trainee, solidifying his stance.

D-Boy and Jay-Roc were victims of Agent Heron's dirty game, where they were merely pawns. Just like in a game of chess, sometimes, the pawn can make it to be a knight or even a king. In this case, D-Boy grew up to be a wise king who took accountability for his mistakes and corrected his future actions. Unfortunately, there's collateral damage that makes this situation worse.

They pulled up to the safe house. D-Boy didn't get a look at who was driving the car until they got out. He couldn't help but stare at Sarah. She wasn't showing yet, but D-Boy knew about the pregnancy with Dirty Redd. She looked at him with disdain because she realized he knew about the baby.

"You remember Agent Sparrow, or to you, Sarah." Heron noticed the stare down D-Boy and Sarah were having.

"Yeah, I remember her very well, and so does Dirty Redd," D-Boy responded.

"American D-Boy, nice to finally meet the real you. The Arab act wasn't cutting it," Sarah snidely responded.

"I wasn't trying to cut it. I was saving my life from devils like you and your organization."

D-Boy's statement about Dirty Redd struck a chord in both Heron and Sarah. It stung Sarah because she secretly still had feelings for Dirty Redd. She was trained not to develop feelings on missions. However, human nature often transcends CIA training. As much as she tried to kill her emotions for Dirty Redd, she couldn't. That. and the fact that she was still carrying his child because she was hesitant to abort the pregnancy.

For Heron, it was the fact that he was falling in love with Sarah, and he knew she was sexing a Black man. Normally, he would disown her after having sexual relations with a Black man, but like Dirty Redd, Heron developed strong feelings for the killer agent. He trained her. She was his protégé. In fact, Heron praised her as one of his best students.

Agent J was standing in the vestibule when they entered the safe house. He immediately searched D-Boy as he walked toward him. Agent J gave him the craziest, murderous expression after roughly frisking D-Boy. It would've scared the average man, but D-Boy had been to hell and back, so nothing planted fear in him.

"What's up with your man?" D-Boy said, referring to Agent J while looking him dead in the eyes.

"This is Agent J. He will be your liaison between us and the Diaz brothers."

"The Diaz brothers? Sounds like a Spanish singing group," D-Boy joked.

"I assure you they are *not* singers. The Diaz brothers are on their way to being the largest cocaine dealers on earth. They created a new, highly potent brand of coke called Nitro. That's where you come in. You're going to assist us in shipping their product to America and delivering it to them. If anything happens, like, you know, John gets involved, Grandpa Joe dies."

D-Boy's mind was racing a million miles a minute. He was angry, but he couldn't show his emotions. He learned a valuable lesson from John in Dubai: *Never let your emotions supersede your intelligence. Be calm under pressure. Then you'll be deadly when it's time to strike.*

"That's what this is about? You don't need me for this. You could've done this without me," D-Boy protested.

"On the contrary, by using you, I don't have to sacrifice

one of my agents for the job. If you get caught, it's on you. I like to keep my hands clean," Heron snickered.

"Your hands will never be clean." D-Boy spoke as if his tongue were a two-edged sword.

"Enough small talk. There's someone dying to see you. I mean that literally."

Heron led D-Boy to a blocked-off section of the safe house with a keypad next to a door. He pressed a four-digit code, and the door slid open. Grandpa Joe was lying in a bed watching TV when he noticed the door opening. Sitting up, he tried to focus on the man entering the room, but his sight was very bad.

As D-Boy got closer, he came into focus. "Grandpa Joe, it's me, D-Boy."

"D-Boy?" he squinted his eyes. "D-Boy is dead!" he shouted.

"The D-Boy that you knew is dead, but your grandson Darius Jensen is alive."

Grandpa Joe slowly stood up and squinted again. This time, he knew exactly who was standing there. "I'll be dammed. That *is* you. D-Boy." He hugged D-Boy with all his might. "I can't believe it's you! Like Jesus rising from the grave, D-Boy is alive!"

"It's me in the flesh. It's good to see you. I missed you, Grandpa Joe." D-Boy shed a tear.

"I missed you too. You know you was my buddy. After you left, your dad came home, and Jay-Roc stepped up and was doing the damn thing with the label and the clothing line. He held the family down while you were gone."

"He was holding me down too, this whole seven years." D-Boy shook his head.

"Damn, it's been seven years since you died-I mean, since you . . . You know what the fuck I mean."

"I know what you mean," D-Boy smiled.

"This is amazing. I knew they couldn't take you out. You a bad motherfucker, D-Boy. The best that ever did it. You came back from the grave on these bitches." Grandpa Joe sat down. "I have to sit. All this excitement is getting me woozy." He paused. "So, where have you been the last seven years?"

"I've been a resident of the United Arab Emirates of Dubai," D-Boy answered.

"Dubai? That's over there in Saudi Arabia or something like that."

"Yeah, it's something like that but more expensive. Because of Jay-Roc, I could live it up for the whole seven years."

"What's this all about? Who the fuck are these weird-ass crackers? The tall one is the crazy one. He's always looking like Frankenstein or some kind of killer robot or something," Grandpa Joe said.

"They are the CIA, and this is all about drug money. They were using me from the start, and when I found out I had two choices—die or go to jail for the rest of my life—I chose death. They're trying to put me back in the game that I literally killed myself to get out of." D-Boy shook his head.

"I was worried, but I'm not now because I know you got a plan." Grandpa Joe winked at D-Boy.

D-Boy winked back and hugged him again so he could whisper in his ear. "I'm going to get us the fuck up out of here." Then he stepped back and smiled. And Grandpa Joe smiled back.

I-75 SOUTH

John had the Warlord on autopilot while he looked up information on the location his tracker was leading him to. Before D-Boy got on the plane headed for Atlanta, he made him swallow a plastic tracking device that dissolves in 24 hours. It was designed to be undetectable from radar long enough to pinpoint a location before self-destruction.

John had their location. He was studying the blueprint of the safe house to devise a plan to free D-Boy and Grandpa Joe. He knew time was of the essence. He needed time to gather more intel. A chill shot up his spine as he was thinking about the Mossad agent he saw at the hospital.

He was a teen when I left Israel 20 years ago, John thought while scratching his chin. *If he's here working with Heron, he has to be a double agent working for Mossad.*

He contemplated that thought and its implications, and it frightened him to his core. John knew way more about the inner workings of the Elite Cabal of Zionists than he cared to know. Before defecting from Mossad, John made it to the top of the food chain of the international intelligence community, which gave him access to information and plans that only a few knew. The more he learned, the more he was convinced he was a pawn. He saw how society was unraveling due to the shift in world politics, world economics, and the social grooming for world domination. He knew who was behind major events, from man-made hurricanes and false flag events to manufactured economic collapse. John knew that The Great Prophecy had begun.

The Great Prophecy was part of the reason he left Mossad. The Great Prophecy was a dystopian future designed by Elite Zionists who were using the religion of Judaism to rule the entire planet. It operates on the notion that the Jews are God's chosen people, but it takes it a bit further. It suggests that every Jewish person shall have at their disposal 200,000 servants . . . for lack of a better word, slaves. Their goal was to enslave the entire world under the premise that Jews were God's chosen people, making the Elite Zionists the masters of the universe.

When John uncovered the true plot of the Great Prophecy, he vowed to destroy any attempts to make it a reality. He destroyed the databank of information on the Elite's plan, which delayed it for the last 20 years, but he couldn't destroy the infrastructure they built to totally take out their plans. He knew one day it would resurface, and his worst nightmares would come true.

John opposed the Great Prophecy from its inception, especially when he learned that the Elite were going to use the ordinary Jews to fulfill their agenda. Then they were going to throw them to the wolves as a scapegoat for throwing the world into perpetual slavery when it really was just a small group of Elite Zionists behind it. In fact, he learned that after the smoke cleared, they were going to kill and enslave the poor Jews after using them to implement their agenda.

John was so deep in thought he didn't notice that he was two minutes away from the location. He immediately sat up, took the wheel, and switched the vehicle from autopilot to manual mode. The location was a house half a mile from the main road, so John just drove past it.

"Time to deploy the drones." He pressed a button, and a surveillance drone concealed in the roof of the Warlord flew out and traveled over the safe house to record and collect intel. The infrared camera detected explosives all along the half-mile road to the safe house. Other explosives were planted around the house. It would be almost impossible to get in without getting blown to bits.

"OK, now, I know not to drive up and rescue them that way, but I'll figure it out. Either way, I will get them out of there alive."

John drove to his Airbnb and parked. The drone followed and landed on the roof in its respective perch. He entered the house and looked at his laptop to plan how he would save his comrades. It wouldn't be easy, but John was determined to complete his mission.

He thought about D-Boy. *Don't worry, I got you, brother.*

CHAPTER 5
THE DIAZ BROTHERS' MANSION, SANDY SPRINGS, GEORGIA

YC STOPPED at the huge iron fence, waiting to be buzzed in. The Diaz brothers' mansion was built like a fortress, with cameras surrounding the entire property. It was highly secured, with attack dogs and armed guards walking the property's perimeter. Fernando put safety and security above all. He knew King Cobra wanted to take them out for defecting from the Lost Souls Cartel. The penalty was death for their transgressions.

YC parked and entered the 15,000 sq. foot estate. Diego and Fernando met him in the foyer. They both had smiles on their faces because they knew what the meeting was about. They finally got the connect to ship their first ton of Nitro into the United States. This was the moment they were all waiting for.

"YC, today is a glorious day," Fernando said as he gave him a handshake and a manly hug.

"I knew you could pull it off." Diego followed suit by shaking his hand, followed by a hug.

"No doubt," YC responded.

"What time will they be here?" Fernando asked.

"They're supposed to be here in an hour."

"Great. Just in time for the game between Colombia and Mexico," Diego said.

YC and the Diaz brothers formed a bond, one that was fortified through the millions of dollars they made together. YC had a motto. Once he made a lot of money with someone, he was loyal to them for life. His father taught him to value strong connections more than childhood friendships. He stuck to that rule and never hung with guys who weren't getting the bag.

"Them cats you grew up with ain't getting no money. Get with some dudes that you can build a bond through getting money. Like minds think alike, and they have the same aspirations. Stay away from broke people, and you won't be like them," YC's father told him.

The three men sat on the couch, having drinks and watching the pregame show. Less than an hour later, the buzzer for the front gate rang. Fernando looked at his phone, which showed who was at the gate. He didn't recognize the two men in the car.

"Identify yourself," he said through the intercom.

"It's Haitian John's people," Agent J said.

"You recognize these cats?" Fernando asked while showing YC his phone.

YC squinted his eyes to focus. "The passenger looks like D-Boy!"

"You sure?" Diego asked.

"I'm positive. I'll never forget his face."

Fernando opened the gate, and the black Benz slowly

entered and parked in the driveway. Agent J and D-Boy casually walked to the door and waited for it to open. YC, Fernando, and Diego were in the foyer to greet their possible new business partners. They were all baffled to know that the mystery man, D-Boy, was in on this transaction. There was some explanation to do because they didn't think he had anything to do with the new plug. But it didn't matter as long as the deal got done.

"What's popping, D-Boy?" Fernando asked with a smile. "We were just talking about you."

"I hope it was good; I don't want no smoke," D-Boy responded.

"What's up, my guy?" Diego asked Agent J.

He was awkward, so he just nodded and said, "I'm good. Let's get down to business."

"That's what I like to hear," Fernando said.

"Here's the address of the warehouse where the ton of Nitro will be delivered. After today, you'll be dealing with D-Boy directly." Agent J gave off weird vibes when he spoke.

"OK. When will the first shipment land?" Diego asked.

"Tomorrow at 3:00 p.m."

"Excellent," Fernando said.

"What happened to Haitian John? I thought he was our guy," Fernando asked.

"Let's just say he 'retired' from the game." Agent J let off a hint of eeriness that was palpable.

YC found that answer unsettling. "You killed him, didn't you? You sick fuck!"

Agent J smiled as if to say, "Yeah, I killed him, and I

enjoyed it." Then he said, "D-Boy will stay here with you until tomorrow to take you to the warehouse and to make sure all is well. Have a good day, gentlemen." Agent J did an about-face and headed for the door.

D-Boy didn't budge. "I see the soccer game between Colombia and Mexico is on. I got heavy into soccer when I lived in Dubai."

Before leaving, Agent J whispered in D-Boy's ear, "Your phone is recording everything. If you say anything about us, your grandfather will die a painful death."

D-Boy just nodded in agreement. Agent J casually exited the mansion and drove back to the safe house.

When he left, YC had a few questions. "What's up with your man? He can't even hide his creepiness."

"First off, he's *not* my mans. He's just a business associate. I feel the same way about him that you do. He's a fucking weirdo creep," D-Boy replied.

"What really happened to Haitian John?" Fernando asked.

"Your guess is as good as mine. All I know is that you have a ton of Nitro landing tomorrow, and I'm facilitating the transaction." D-Boy redirected the interrogation because he knew the conversation was being monitored.

"It's all good. Let's celebrate!" Diego poured some Ace of Spades Champagne into four champagne flutes and lifted his glass in the air. "To a new, successful partnership and the Diaz Cartel."

The men raised their glasses and made the toast. D-Boy was the only one who wasn't feeling festive about the situation. He had made a vow never to get involved with drugs again. The seven years in Dubai changed his life. He saw the destruction he did to his community and hated what he did. Being forced to participate in this deal hurt his spirit on levels that made him feel defeated. But he had to remain strong for Grandpa Joe.

THE SAFE HOUSE

Sarah was in the bathroom throwing up again. Her pregnancy was making her sick. She wasn't showing that much because she was naturally petite. But soon, she would be, and she would have to decide whether to abort the child. She was on the fence about terminating the pregnancy because she was secretly in love with Dirty Redd. She knew it was against the Agency's policy, but she couldn't help what she was feeling.

She often sat and thought about the time she spent with him and all the great sex they had. Part of getting him to be enticed was having excessive sex with him. Her training taught her to cut off her emotions on missions like this. She wasn't supposed to fall in love. She fought hard not to think about Dirty Redd, but to no avail, because everything reminded her of him.

She also knew that Heron was in love with her. They were spending more time together since the mission was over. He was obsessed with her and wanted to have daily sex with her, sometimes three times a day. She wasn't into him, but she played the game because she knew rejecting him could result in her demise.

Heron was sadistic, especially when he didn't get his

way. The Agency would often dispose of agents who went against the rules. Heron would kill her in the blink of an eye if he knew the truth that she was in love with a Black man. He was a staunch racist who opposed interracial relationships, let alone a biracial baby.

She wanted to keep the baby because of her love of Dirty Redd, but keeping the baby was a risk to her life and the baby's, so she had to play the game. Her plan was simple yet complex. She made up her mind to keep her baby.

"Are you OK in there?" Heron asked after hearing her throwing up again. "You must have a virus or something because you've been throwing up daily for the past week."

She opened the bathroom door and gave Heron a concerned look. "There's something I have to tell you."

"Go ahead and spit it out."

"Well, there's no easy way to say this, but I think I'm pregnant."

Heron smiled. "You're pregnant?"

"That's why I've been sick every morning."

"I've always wanted a son to fulfill my legacy." He hugged her tightly. "This would mean the world to me if you were to have my child." Heron got misty-eyed at the thought.

"Hold your horses. What if it's a girl?" Sarah replied.

"Whatever you have, I will love and provide for you and the child." Heron wiped away the tears of joy.

"I'm so happy that you want to have this baby because I know Agency policy when it comes to having babies by agents," Sarah said.

"Fuck what the Agency has to say. We can retire and ride off into the sunset." Heron was a wishful thinker because he knew the Agency wasn't going for that.

"You and I both know it won't be that easy." Sarah's expression showed concern.

"I have some pull at the top with the director. He owes me a few favors."

Sarah hugged him while whispering, "I love you so much."

"*Dirty Redd*," Sarah screamed in her head.

"I love you more. I'm going to take care of it; don't worry about the Agency. You just relax from now on. I'm putting you on light duty so you and the baby will be stress free," Heron said.

"Thank you, baby. I'm going to lie down and get some rest."

As she walked to her room, Agent J walked in from the meeting with the Diaz brothers. Sarah walked past him without saying a word. She didn't care for him. She felt his creepiness. She knew he was a coldhearted killer, unlike most of the agents who only kill if they had to. But to him, it was a hobby. The Agency called Agent J's type "Beast."

Agent J knew how most people felt about him, and he didn't care. In his mind, if you weren't Jewish, then you were goyim, which in Hebrew was equivalent to "human scum." His true mission was to carry out the Great Prophecy. He was on standby awaiting orders. For now, he played the role because, at any given time, he would murder everyone in the safe house if instructed to.

Heron greeted Agent J. "How did the meeting with the Diaz brothers go?"

"Everything is going according to plan. I left D-Boy with them as directed, and they'll receive the package." Agent J never showed emotion when he spoke.

"Excellent. We're in business with the Diaz brothers. Now, we have to get rid of the Lost Souls Cartel before they take out the Diaz brothers."

"I would love to murder King Cobra with my bare hands," Agent J said with his signature evil scowl.

"I know, but this one has to be hands-off. I'm going to send in the drones to bomb his whole compound. That way, he won't see it coming. He has an army protecting him, so it won't be easy to just '*kill him with your bare hands.*'" Heron mocked Agent J's request to murder King Cobra.

Agent J nodded in agreement. "Got you." Then he dismissed himself.

I can't wait to kill you with my bare hands, Heron, Agent J thought as he walked to his room.

Heron walked to the part of the house where Grandpa Joe was captive. He pressed the code to unlock the door. "What's up, my nigga?" Heron spoke with a mock street accent.

"I'm not your nigga, you fucking cracker," Grandpa Joe said with venom.

"Come on, Joe, that's no way to speak to the man who holds your life in his hands, now, is it?"

Grandpa Joe thought about his next statement. "I'm hungry. I haven't eaten since yesterday. I feel my sugar getting low."

"What do you want to eat today?" Heron asked.

"They got Boston Market around here?" Grandpa Joe asked.

"OF course. If that's what my nigga wants, that's what my nigga gets. I was just checking on you to make sure you're still alive. I wouldn't want anything to happen to my main nigga. Know what I mean?"

Fuck you, you fucking cracker devil, Grandpa Joe thought.

"Yeah, I know what you mean," Grandpa Joe said as he lay on the bed, grabbed the remote, and began flicking through the channels on the flat screen.

"Good boy," Heron said, exiting the room. "I'm going to enjoy killing that old nigga myself after I kill his grandson, D-Boy."

Heron walked to his office and looked at his laptop screen, which showed the schematics of the Lost Souls compound, "I'm about to decimate you, King Cobra." Heron reveled in the thought of his plans to destroy the cartel.

Immediately, his cell phone rang. It was the commander in charge of the drone strike. "Special Agent Heron, this is Commander Lewis calling to inform you that you have been green-lit for your request to strike the site known as The Lost Souls compound at 16:00 hours tomorrow. The link to view it live will be sent to your secure email address."

"Thank you, Commander. I'll have my popcorn ready for the movie."

"I'm sure you will," the commander responded before hanging up.

Heron reached for the expensive cigar box, grabbed one, and lit it up. Then he sat back in his chair before exhaling the smoke. He thought about his last meeting with

King Cobra. It was a charade of kindness and partnership coming from Heron because he knew that day would be the last day he would lay eyes on the cartel boss.

He looked at the intel picture of King Cobra on the screen, took another long drag of the cigar, and exhaled. "Adios, amigos."

CHAPTER 6
LOST SOULS CARTEL COMPOUND. CALI, COLOMBIA

KING COBRA WAS SURROUNDED by 10 of his top guards. He knew he was going to be under attack by the CIA any day now because Agent Heron cut off all communication with him. He had the inside scoop that Heron traded in the product from The Lost Souls for Nitro from the Diaz brothers. He knew that the Diaz brothers were growing their own cocaine that was sweeping the nation. He couldn't compete with the potency of their product, so his grip on the market was slowly waning.

King Cobra studied U.S. relations with the cartels. He learned they had a history of flipping the script and quickly turning the tables. One day, you were their partners, and the next, you were put on the terrorist watch list. It usually means they were going to assassinate you when they're done with you. They left no loose ends that could come back to haunt them.

King Cobra had deep tunnels built under the compound for escape. He was living life on the edge because he knew they would strike any day, and when they did, it would be catastrophic for the Lost Souls Cartel. But he wasn't going down without a fight. His army was fully armed and ready to fight back.

"Where is Rodolfo?" Rodolfo was still King Cobra's second in command. King Cobra killed every lieutenant he appointed, but Rodolfo lasted the longest, which was five years.

Rodolfo was right by King Cobra's side so quickly it seemed like a magic trick. "I'm right here, King Cobra, sir."

"Did you find the secret location of the Diaz brothers' headquarters in the United States?" King Cobra asked.

"Not yet. But my sources in the U.S. said they are getting close to finding their location," Nervous, Rodolfo answered. He knew King Cobra could murder him at the drop of a dime.

Suddenly, King Cobra threw a tantrum, knocking weapons off a table and kicking boxes. "What the fuck you mean they couldn't find the exact location? I paid $100K to find them, but they still haven't done the job."

"We know they're in Georgia. Any day, we'll narrow it down to the exact area," Rodolfo answered.

At that moment, all the men in the room stood still at the sound of a loud whistle coming from the sky. "What the fuck is that noise?" King Cobra asked.

"Get down!" Rodolfo shouted. "It's a drone strike!"

"Go to the tunnel!" King Cobra commanded.

The tunnel was about 50 yards from the building they were in. Getting there safely under a drone strike was going to be difficult. Just as they exited the building, a missile hit it, and it exploded, killing two of the men accompanying King Cobra. The other men didn't look back as they raced. They all made it to the opening of the underground tunnel and entered it as fast as possible before the next missile hit. As the last man entered the tunnel entrance, a missile hit the area, but the men were already deep underground and weren't affected by the blast.

"This way!" Rodolfo instructed the men.

They ran through the tunnel as quickly as they could. As they ran, the ground shook, and the tunnel ceiling collapsed behind them. The CIA knew the tunnel was there, and they were hitting it with a bunker-busting missile that was designed to burrow itself underground before exploding. The fire from the explosion created a vacuum of heat that would travel through the entire tunnel, scorching anything in its path.

Besides King Cobra and Rodolfo, there were eight men. The exit hatch to the tunnel was about 100 yards. The bunker-buster hit and exploded, giving them 20 seconds to reach the exit before they were all incinerated. King Cobra and Rodolfo were at the head of the line, so they would be the first to exit. When the missile exploded, they felt the heat as the fire traveled through the interior.

"Hurry! The fire is coming!" Rodolfo shouted to King Cobra.

King Cobra reached the exit and quickly raced up the ladder to the escape hatch. He made it through the opening. Looking behind him, he saw six of his men escaping. Two of his soldiers met their horrific demise as the blast caught them before they could escape. As the six men reached the surface, so did an explosion of fire. Fortunately, the flames did not touch them. They made it out alive.

Rodolfo ran to a wooded area where two four-door camouflaged Wranglers were covered by a tarp that hid them in the bushes. All the men quickly jumped into the Jeeps and drove off. Although the drone strike hit hard and fast, King Cobra escaped with six elite soldiers and Rodolfo.

"Nice fucking try, Agent Heron! It's not that easy to take out the King Cobra, you motherfucker." King Cobra shouted out in victory of the failed assassination attempt.

"Let's not count the chickens before they hatch. The drones are still scanning the area for anything moving. We have only minutes to make it to the underground compound, or the drone will strike the vehicles," Rodolfo said.

The drones were in an area 20,000 feet high, doing a quick scan of the area to see if there were any signs of life using infrared technology. They could distinguish between injured and dead bodies on the compound. The injured showed a faint red light, while the dead bodies showed blue, which meant the body was cold with no life force energy left. Some 876 men died and 107 injured. The drone was now expanding its search to see if anyone had escaped.

This gave King Cobra and his few men minutes to reach the secret underground compound about five more miles east of the main compound. They sped at 85 miles an hour through the makeshift pathway. The drones were miles from them, and Heron's intel didn't reveal the secret underground compound. However, if the drones caught up with them, it would record them entering the subterranean facility.

They were still yards from the hidden entrance, and the drones were seconds from being able to see them. Rodolfo pressed the automatic opening to the compound as a drone moved fast in the same direction. In seconds, the drone would see them and blast them with hellfire missiles that would destroy anything in its path. Hellfire missiles were known for their deadly accuracy.

As the two Wranglers approached the entrance, the drone's surveillance camera was just a mere fraction of a second behind them. But as the drone finally came in viewing distance, the second Wrangler's rear bumper disappeared into the entrance, and the secret opening closed. The drone kept flying east, past the entrance of the hidden compound, looking for any survivors.

"I think we got them all, sir," the drone pilot reported to Agent Heron.

"Double back one more time just to make sure. You know how sneaky snakes are. We don't want to take no chances leaving King Cobra alive to bite us in the ass," Heron responded.

"I got you, sir." The pilot flew the drone back west and did another sweep of the area before reporting, "I think that's it. There's no indication of any life force in the area."

"OK, get out of the area before Colombia's Air Force detects you."

They had obliterated the Lost Souls compound. The only building left standing was the cocaine-processing plant. Heron knew there would be a ton or two of cocaine there for the taking. He has already instructed a standby group of CIA operatives in the area to go in and retrieve the cocaine left there. Heron was always finding ways to manipulate the situation. He had an unwitting dope boy in several major cities waiting for him to supply them with major weight.

"All in a day's work," Heron said as he lit up the Cuban cigar and took two pulls before putting it out and making a call. It rang twice before D-Boy picked up. "My nigga, D, what's up?"

"Come on with the fake Black guy act. You've been doing that corny shit since I met you 10 years ago. Don't you get tired of being a fucking looser?" D-Boy spoke from the heart, and Heron felt it. Heron's weakness was being defied. Since he always felt like he had the upper hand, he felt like no one was in a position to respond, or they'd lose their life. He quickly learned that the Jensens were a different breed. They didn't give a fuck about authority, dating back to slavery.

"You know that's no way to talk to the man who has your grandfather's life in his hands, now, is it?"

D-Boy took a deep breath. "What's up? I know you're not calling to see how my day is going."

"I want you to relay some good news to the Diaz brothers." Heron paused for effect, knowing it was annoying. "King Cobra is dead. I just finished bombing the Lost Souls compound, and we know King Cobra was there."

"Is that all?" D-Boy was noticeably agitated.

"Let's see." He paused again, smiling, knowing its effect.

D-Boy shook his head. *I can't wait to kill this devil!* he thought.

"Oh yeah, find out how much of that last shipment has been moved so I'll know when the next load should be ready."

"I can tell you the answer to that now. They moved half of that ton already," D-Boy reported.

"You got to be kidding me. They just got that shipment less than a month ago."

"On the first day, they had back orders of 300 kilos. This Nitro is like crack in the '80s, only on steroids."

Heron lit his cigar back up and smiled after exhaling the smoke. "You know something, D-Boy? All jokes aside, I miss doing business with you. You were the first nigga that I made into a kingpin. You can say you were the baby of this operation. After you killed yourself, I was devasted. All that money—gone. So I said to myself, 'Why not create a hundred D-Boys all around the country, one in every ghetto?'" Heron marveled at his diabolical creation.

D-Boy was disgusted by his statements. He was 15 years old when Heron approached him and Jason on the block. D-Boy remembered it like it was yesterday. From the first day he met Heron, he was skeptical, but they were desperate and needed a come-up. Little did they know meeting Heron was a Trojan horse. A gift and a curse, one that made D-Boy filthy rich and a marked man simultaneously.

"If I had a chance to do it all again, I would've murdered you on day one. Knowing what I know now, you are the scourge of planet Earth, an evil plague devouring my people. I've come a long way from that little boy on the block and vowed never to return to my old ways. Again, I find myself your victim and your wicked system that continues to destroy lives with the drugs you bring into my community." D-Boy's eyes welled up with water, and he didn't want to spill it down his cheeks, but he couldn't control it. The tears rolled down his face as if his eyelids were the dam, and they just broke.

Heron put out his cigar, jumped to his feet, and began to clap his hands. "Bravo! Bravo! That was very impressive. You said that from the heart, and I felt every word. You're right. You did come a long way since that little nigga on the corner. I'm the one who took you and turned you into D-Boy." He paused. "I'm going to let you in on a little secret. The NYPD was investigating you and your brother for petty drug dealing. You were about to go down to make room in that neighborhood for my operation to work. The NYPD was working with me, not knowing my real plan was to clear that block so I could place my own workers there. I'm the one that stepped in and called them off from arresting you and your brother and creating the lane for you to sell all my drugs, and we got rich. So, before you go acting self-righteous, remember, nigga, *I* made you!" Heron hung up.

D-Boy wiped his tears, and his heart grew cold. He realized he had a big role in his evolution into D-Boy. Heron was right. He gave him the proposal, but he didn't have to take it. It was embedded in him from his upbringing to be a hustler. All he knew growing up was to get money or die trying.

D-Boy exited the plush room, looking for Fernando and Diego to tell them the good news. They were by the pool, surrounded by seven beautiful women in bikinis. They were all fixed on D-Boy when he strolled out onto the deck.

"Ladies, this is my friend, D-Boy," Fernando announced.

"Hi, D-Boy," the ladies said melodically in unison like they were singing a song.

"I have some good news. King Cobra is no more. His compound was just bombed," D-Boy said.

Fernando and Diego smiled and gave each other a handshake and a hug.

"You know what this means?" Diego said.

"There's no competition. We will be the biggest cartel on the planet," Fernando answered.

"This is cause for a celebration," Diego shouted.

All the women clapped their hands, shouting, "Yeah."

The moment eased D-Boy's spirits from the conversation he had with Heron. He needed to relax, so what better way than to celebrate a victory with your new associates? D-Boy saw something in the Diaz brothers that he saw in himself when he was in the game: Ambition. They were willing to go that extra mile to prove a point, and that's why they were winning.

Fernando got on the phone to call YC. "My brother, come through. We're going to throw a party to celebrate the championship."

"What championship?" YC smiled at the gleeful energy coming from his partner.

"Just come over." Fernando hung up the phone.

YC looked at his phone, removed the headphones, and hung them on the microphone stand before him. He was in a soundproof booth recording songs for his new album. The engineer was confused because he was in the middle of the verse.

"What are we doing?" the engineer asked.

"We can finish this tomorrow. I got some shit I gotta take care of." YC gave the engineer a handshake before exiting the studio.

When YC reached his car, he took out a phone with news clippings of an article about Darius "D-Boy" Jensen. He read the article and looked at the picture, but the face in the photo was different from the person he met. Something else caught his attention. It was the last name, Jensen.

His father would tell him he had some family members from Queens, New York, called the Jensens. He remembered his father telling him the story before he died:

"Man, my family on my mother's side, the Jensens . . . They are said to have hustled from the days of slavery. I visited Jamaica Queens for the summers, and as a kid, I made a hundred a day running to the store for my big cousin Joe Jensen. He was the biggest heroin dealer and numbers man in the neighborhood at the time. I would've stayed if my mother had let me. That's where we get our supreme hustling skills. It's in our blood. If it ain't in you, it ain't in you."

YC looked at his phone again and wondered why he felt this was the same Jensen his father had talked about. His intuition told him it meant one thing: if it was the same D-Boy, he was alive; if it was not, he felt the same conclusion.

"Something always been fishy about this guy, but not in a bad way."

From what he read in the articles, D-Boy was legendary in his New York hood. YC admired D-Boy's accomplishments with the clothing line and the record label. He saw the similarities they had in life. YC was a drug-dealing major rapper. He also remembered the energy they shared when he first met him. It was that of a kindred spirit.

He was going to the Diaz brothers' mansion and knew D-Boy was there. This was his opportunity to ask him just to see if he was the same person. There were a lot of Black men from hoods all over America with the name "D-Boy." But one with the last name Jensen and from Queens? YC was about to find out.

In no time, YC pulled up to the mansion in his favorite car, his signature Rolls-Royce Wraith. The driveway looked like a luxury car lot. Carlos and a few of his men pulled up in the latest Mercedes-Benz S580 and BMW 750i. Of course, Fernando's Rolls-Royce and Lamborghini were parked there, and the Ferrari and Bentley belonged to Diego.

YC rang the doorbell and was greeted by Fernando. "My brother from another mother." He gave YC a manly hug and a handshake.

"What's popping, mi amigo? I was in the studio when you called but rushed here to hear the good news in person," YC replied.

"King Cobra is dead. There was a drone strike on his compound; no life was left. The Lost Souls Cartel is finished. That leaves the Diaz brothers as the top contender of cartels." Fernando spoke like a boxer talking to the commentator after a win by knockout.

"Damn, that's good fucking news." YC hugged Fernando again. "Congratulations, my G."

"Now, we can produce more Nitro without the Lost Souls trying to burn down our crops. We can grow 10 times more with them out of the way."

As Fernando spoke, Carlos, Diego, and D-Boy strolled up to them in the foyer. They all gave YC the same hug and handshake except D-Boy. He just gave him a handshake. D-Boy wasn't with all the hugging. He was reserved about showing love because he never knew when he had to flip the script. He was only associated with the Diaz Brothers' Cartel because Heron was forcing him to do so; if not that, he wouldn't have anything to do with them.

D-Boy knew how to blend in without seeming standoffish. He didn't want to throw off the energy of the occasion, so he joined in with the energy. He despised what the Diaz brothers' whole operation stood for. They were picking up where D-Boy left off with the CIA but on a more massive scale. That's what was bothering D-Boy. His having something to do with this operation contradicted his newfound philosophy. He was totally against the selling and distribution of drugs.

The doorbell rang again. "That must be the new batch of beauties I ordered." Fernando answered the door, and there stood seven blindfolded women. He had them all picked up at a local Publix supermarket and blindfolded before they arrived at the mansion's location. He also had their phones taped around the camera section. They could use their phones to make calls, but no pictures or live recordings were allowed.

Now a total of 14 gorgeous women and only eight men were present. So, there were two women for each man, and one of the men had to share to make it even. Because of the women's energy and willingness to entertain the men, the atmosphere was perfect for a good time.

"Don't be shy, fellows. These women are RAW! Ready,

Able, and Willing to do whatever you desire," Diego announced, seeing the divide between the sexes.

The ladies made the first move toward the men. Two women casually approached each man and grabbed him on each arm. The soldier with no woman teamed up with the last trio to make it even. Now that everyone was paired off, the DJ cranked up the system to make it official.

Everyone comfortably sat around the pool, drinking and chatting. Some women sniffed the hill of Nitro being passed around on a silver platter. No member of the Diaz Brothers' Cartel was allowed to use Nitro or the penalty was expulsion from the organization . . . which ultimately resulted in the members being unalive.

YC made sure he sat next to D-Boy so he could spark up a conversation.

"My nigga, D-Boy," YC said in a welcoming tone, "what you been up to, my boi?"

"You know, getting to the bag and staying sucker-free in a world full of lollipops, ya hear?" D-Boy replied.

"I like that, staying sucker-free in a world full of lollipops. I will use that in one of my new songs," YC informed D-Boy.

D-Boy gave YC a handshake. "You got it, baby bro. I got a hundred of those." D-Boy took a healthy swig of his drink.

"Good looking, Unc." YC took a swig before continuing. "You want to know something crazy?"

"What's that?" D-Boy didn't like sentences that started like that.

"Before my pops died, he told me that we had family on

my grandmother's side up in New York with the last name Jensen." YC noticed the switch in D-Boy's energy.

D-Boy turned his head and gave YC a serious look. "My last name is Jenkins, but what part of New York are they from?" he asked out of curiosity.

The woman on D-Boy's right arm saw that he was distracted from his drink, so she put a pinch of Nitro in it. She noticed that he wasn't using it, and Nitro had a hyper-sexual side effect on first-time users. She knew it would make him lust for her once it was time for her to seduce him.

"He said they were from Jamaica Queens; his second cousin Joe Jensen used to get money. He said he used to visit when he was a kid, so you know it was in the '70s."

He's talking about Grandpa Joe. This man is my cousin, but I can't let hm know yet for his own safety, D-Boy thought.

"I heard of the Jensens from Jamaica Queens; every-body heard of them." D-Boy took another swig. "You prob-ably getting me mixed up with the D-Boy from Jamaica Queens. I'm the D-Boy from Brooklyn." D-Boy took the last sip of his drink. "I need another drink." He got up and went to the bar.

YC followed him with his eyes, thinking. *I know bull-shit when I smell it. He's hiding something, and I'm going to find it.*

When D-Boy got up to get his drink, the woman who laced his drink picked up her phone to reread the text before looking at the pictures of Fernando and Diego. The text read: These are the Diaz brothers. I have a $100K reward for anyone who can get me the location of their headquarters in the United States.

She looked across the pool where Fernando and Diego stood and then at their pictures on her phone. "Yeah, that's them, all right," she said, confirming their identity. "I'm about to get that money." She called the number attached to the text. "I'm here at the Diaz brothers' mansion. Is that $100K reward still there for the location?"

"Yes!" Rodolfo got up and knocked on King Cobra's door. He quickly opened it and came face-to-face with Rodolfo. "You'll get the money once you can confirm it's actually their location and take a pic of the Diaz brothers for proof."

The woman knew she couldn't get pictures of them because she would look suspect and would probably get killed if they caught her. She thought fast. She wanted that reward money to pay for her BBL body job to enhance her looks. She didn't know the address, and she couldn't take pictures.

"I got it. I'm going to share my location with you. That way, you will have the exact location of their mansion."

"Well, what are you waiting for? Start sharing!" Rodolfo replied impatiently.

The woman saw D-Boy returning to the chair he had been sitting in, which was right beside her. She nervously fumbled with the phone while trying to pull up the feature on her phone that would share her location before D-Boy sat down beside her. She was feeling the effects of the alcohol and the Nitro mix and suddenly felt super high. She never sniffed that much Nitro before because she couldn't afford more than the small amounts.

"Oh shit, I'm so fucking high," she said into the phone.

"Fuck that. Hurry up and share the fucking location, stupid bitch," Rodolfo yelled, growing more impatient by the second.

"I'm trying." She pressed a button, and the "share my location" prompt appeared. But just as she was about to hit the button, her cell phone died, and all communication ended. "Fuck, I needed that."

"You needed what?" D-Boy asked.

She was caught off guard, and D-Boy sensed it. "Oh, nothing. Somebody tried to Cash App me a few hundred dollars, but my phone died."

"Don't worry. I got you," D-Boy slurred. "What's your name?"

"My name is Dalia, and what's your name?" she asked.

"They call me D-Boy."

She looked at him with her seductive, hazel eyes and grabbed his penis. "Nice to meet you, D-Boy. I want to provide you with the ultimate pleasure." She puckered up her full lips and slowly kissed his face. Then she moved to his lips when she sensed his approval.

D-Boy kissed the back of her hand. "The pleasure is all mines." The hypersexual effect of Nitro was kicking in. D-Boy found himself not being able to control his attraction to Dalia.

The woman on his left arm joined in and began kissing his face and grabbing his penis as it started to throb in their grip. Now, D-Boy was feeling the full effects of the powerful narcotic. It wasn't enough to get him addicted, just enough to get him knocked off his square. D-Boy never did drugs, so this was feeling extra good to him.

Dalia pulled out D-Boy's manhood and started giving him fellatio under the table. The second girl rubbed on his body, awaiting her turn. When Dalia came up for air, girl number 2 went under the table like she was going under water.

Next, the whole party erupted into a sex fest. All the beautiful women were on their knees, sucking and licking on the men and kissing each other. It got wild so fast that D-Boy didn't know what was happening, but he was always on point. He sold drugs his whole life and was able to make it by following the golden rule: NEVER get high off your own supply!

His head lay back as the women took turns salivating on him, but after a few minutes, he opened his eyes and shook his head. "Wait a minute! What the fuck is going on?" He stood up and put his dick back in his pants. "I got a room. I don't get down with the freak-offs out in the open." He started walking toward his room in the spacious mansion, the girls in tow. When he got to his room, they both attacked him like he was a piece of filet mignon, and they were wolves that hadn't eaten in a month.

"Take it easy!" D-Boy protested.

Dalia paused and took out her cell phone. "Shit, I need a charger," she said. She looked around the room, and right by the bed was a phone charger. She quickly crossed the room and connected her phone to the charger while the other woman was satisfying D-Boy. She was back so fast they didn't notice it.

"Where was I?" Dalia said before she got on her knees to join in the fun.

CHAPTER 7
THE DIAZ BROTHERS' MANSION

THE SUN WAS RISING when D-Boy opened his eyes. He looked, and in both arms was a beautiful woman. *What the fuck?* He thought he was dreaming because he couldn't remember what happened last night.

He sat up in the bed while the two women still slept. He closed his eyes and tried to recall all the events. Slowly, visions of the night started coming into focus. Everything slowly came back to him.

The celebration was because of King Cobra. Yeah, that's what happened. All the girls came in blindfolded, and then they started sucking me. D-Boy jumped up. "I didn't use a condom!"

He went to the shower and felt disgusted with himself. While he was washing, he tried to understand why he was feeling this way. He was in tune with his mind, and something wasn't connecting. He knew himself. He never got drunk to the point where he wasn't in control.

"I must have been drugged," he concluded. "When?"

He tried to recall when he left his drink unattended. He remembered his conversation with YC about him being his cousin. He remembered turning to give him his full attention.

It could've been at that moment because YC caught me off guard. I need to check in with John, D-Boy thought.

When he entered the room to get his phone, he saw Dalia grabbing her phone off the charger. He watched her as she tried to make a call, to no avail. "Come on, pick up. I need that reward money." She spoke low, trying not to be heard, but D-Boy heard her loud and clear. She was desperate to give King Cobra some information so she could collect the money.

Reward money? D-Boy thought.

He had a flashback from last night when Dalia was on the phone.

"Fuck, I needed that."

"You needed what?" D-Boy asked.

She was caught off guard, and D-Boy sensed it. "Oh, nothing. Somebody tried to Cash App me a few hundred dollars, but my phone died."

"Don't worry, I got you," D-Boy slurred, "What's your name?"

"My name is Dalia, and what's your name?" she asked.

"They call me D-Boy."

That's when things went blank, and she started seducing me. It's all starting to make sense, D-Boy thought.

While she was trying to make the call, D-Boy quietly grabbed his gun. "Drop the phone before I blow your fucking brains out."

She immediately dropped the phone. "Please, don't shoot me!"

"Sit on your hands."

She complied.

"Who the fuck are you trying to call? And what is the reward money?" he cocked back the hammer. "And don't fucking lie."

"OK." Dalia took a deep breath. "I was calling a guy from the Lost Souls Cartel. They put out a text that they have a $100K reward for anyone that can give them the location of the Diaz brothers' headquarters."

"Did you give them the location?"

"I couldn't share my location with them because my phone died last night."

Her phone rang.

"Who is it?" He paused while she looked at the caller ID.

"It's the guy from the Lost Souls," she confirmed.

D-Boy thought fast. "Pick up and tell them you'll have the location in half an hour."

"Do you have the location?" Rodolfo asked.

"I'll call you back with the location in half an hour."

"What the fuck do you mean you'll have it in 30 minutes?" Rodolfo responded angrily.

"Just pick up in 30 minutes." She hung up.

"Good girl. Now, get the fuck up. You're coming with me."

D-Boy walked her to Fernando's quarters and knocked on the door.

"Who is it?"

"It's D-Boy. We have a serious situation we need to deal with ASAP," he said through the bedroom door.

Fernando got up and put on his Versace robe. When he opened the door, D-Boy was standing there holding Dalia's arm with a gun pointed at her head. Fernando automatically knew this was a serious situation. He moved to the side to let them in.

"What's going on?"

"I'll let her tell you." He paused. "Go ahead, spit it out."

"I was trying to call a member of the Lost Souls cartel to get the reward money for giving up your location."

Fernando snatched the phone out of her hand and read the message. "Nice try, *cabrón* (bastard)." He smiled.

"I think we should give him a fake location and ambush them when they show up," D-Boy suggested.

Fernando scratched his chin. "That's a brilliant idea. I have a house I just bought in Marietta. Here's the address: 3400 Main Station Ave. Give it to him." Fernando rushed to get dressed and got on his phone, "Carlos, get the squad ready. We got some smoke to air out."

Dalia texted the address to Rodolfo and then called him. "That's the address to the headquarters." She hung up. "Can I go now?"

D-Boy looked at her and then at Fernando. It was his call whether she lived or died at this moment.

"Keep an eye on her until this is over," he told D-Boy.

"I got you." D-Boy escorted her back to his room.

"What the hell did I get myself into?" Dalia asked herself out loud.

"You just got yourself into some deep shit." D-Boy

knew it was up to the Diaz brothers if she would live to see another day. He took her stylish Fendi scarf and used it to tie her hands around the thick wooden bedpost. "Don't even try to get loose because this knot is designed to tighten if you attempt to untie it."

"OK. I'm not going to try to get loose if you promise me more of your delicious cock."

"I'm good on that. In fact, that's the last thing you should be worried about."

D-Boy went to the balcony to call John on a secure encrypted line. "I will send you a phone number to tap into." D-Boy pulled out Dalia's phone and texted the number to John.

"OK, got it." Just that fast, John's supercomputer could pinpoint the phone's location and listen to all conversations. He could also turn the phone's camera on and off.

"They're sending a 10-man team to 3400 Main Station Ave. in Marietta. Their ETA is 35 minutes." John looked at the blueprint of the house. "Place three men in the house, shooting from the second floor just to draw them in. Then have another three-man team ambush them from behind after they're drawn in from the firefight coming from the house," John instructed D-Boy.

"That's why I fuck with you. You always got a plan."

"Put your earpiece in, and I'll guide you from my end," John said.

"Got you."

D-Boy hung up and got with the six-man team. "Listen, there's only six of us, so here's the plan."

"What about what's-her-name? Should I just kill her?" Diego asked.

"Not yet. She's useful for now," D-Boy answered. "She's tied up to the bed. Put one of your trained dogs by the door."

After Diego put the massive Rottweiler by the door, D-Boy laid out the plan given to him by John. The fake mansion was only 15 minutes away, so they were there 15 minutes ahead of the Lost Soul soldiers. That gave them time to set up for their arrival.

KING COBRA'S UNDERGROUND COMPOUND. COLOMBIA

Rodolfo was scrolling through his contacts, looking for Lost Soul soldiers in the Georgia area. That was the one thing that the CIA didn't destroy . . . King Cobra's vast network of operatives dispersed throughout the United States. King Cobra saw it as the perfect contingency plan in the event that something like this happened, and it did. This move put him two moves ahead of his enemies, both the Diaz brothers and Agent Heron.

In no time, Rodolfo had contacted 10 Lost Soul soldiers within a 25-mile radius of the location. They were headed there fast; they all would arrive around the same time. Their mission was to eliminate the Diaz brothers. Without them, there was no Diaz Brothers' Cartel, and King Cobra knew this. They didn't have enough time to raise successors to their baby empire.

"I have a 10-man team converging on that location, King Cobra, sir. Their ETA is 35 minutes," Rodolfo informed him.

"I want them reporting in real time."

"Yes, King Cobra, sir," Rodolfo replied.

The time flew by as if this event were a championship game. Both sides are anxious to kill and win the game of King of the Cartel. The Diaz brothers were the underdogs, while the Lost Souls were the favorite. However, the Diaz brothers had a smaller organization, but they had one thing that gave them the advantage: John Gillespie.

"They should be coming to the address in three minutes," Rodolfo reported.

"I don't have to be there to touch you, fucking cockroach. You think you're going to go to America with *my* money and resources and start your own cartel? Not while I'm alive," King Cobra yelled.

DIAZ BROTHERS' ESTATE IN MARIETTA, GEORGIA

D-Boy set up the ambush the way that John instructed. He put the soldiers in the house on the second floor, one in the middle, and the other two on the west and east wing of the house. Their job was to initiate a gunfight with the Lost Souls. As soon as they moved in, D-Boy, Fernando, and Diego would flank them from behind and kill them.

"They will be there in approximately two minutes," John reported.

"We're ready," D-Boy replied.

At that exact time, three SUVs pulled up, and 10 soldiers hopped out with guns ready. Before they could let off a shot, the three men in the house started firing at them. The Lost Souls fired back in a staccato of gunfire. Two of the Lost Souls were hit but still firing on the house.

"Wait for it," John instructed. "Let them move in a few more feet—NOW!"

D-Boy was the first to move. "Let's go!"

The three of them began shooting with automatic gunfire at the backs of the Lost Souls. Five of the men were hit instantly, and the other five ran toward the house, which is what John anticipated they would do. Two more of the men were hit by bullets coming from the house. The last three put down their weapons and surrendered.

"*No mas!*" one of the men yelled out. "*Perdoname la vida!*" he yelled out. (No more! Spare my life!)

"Don't shoot them," Fernando ordered.

The three soldiers exited the house with their guns aimed at the three surviving Lost Souls soldiers. They stood with their hands high in the air, praying to themselves that no one would kill them on the spot. Fernando walked up to them and paused for a few seconds. He recognized them from his tenure as a Lost Soul soldier.

"I remember you. Your name is Juan; he is Henry, and you are José." Fernando had a total recall moment.

"We went on missions together for the cartel, remember?" Juan replied.

"I remember these two," Diego pointed to Henry and José. "We played soccer together."

"I would kill you, but I know what it's like working for a tyrant like King Cobra. He doesn't care about you, just like he didn't care about my uncle Captain Diaz; God rest his soul."

"I miss Captain Diaz. He taught me how to be a soldier. The whole cartel thought that it was wrong of King Cobra to kill him like that," Juan added.

Fernando paused because he was in deep thought. "I'm going to allow you to work for the Diaz brothers. We will treat you as an equal, and we make sure all of our members are paid well, unlike King Cobra."

The three men looked at each other as if it were a no-brainer. "*Si, trabajaremos para uste*," (Yes, we will work for you) Juan promised.

"I think that was a good choice for the Diaz brothers," John told D-Boy.

"I'm curious. Why?" D-Boy asked.

"A former enemy will be more loyal than a recruited soldier because he has more to prove. Hannibal replenished his diminished army after crossing the Alps by recruiting the Sicilians, who were his sworn enemy. They went on to fight valiantly for him," John said to D-Boy through his earpiece, which no one else could hear.

"Let's get out of here before the Georgia State Troopers come," D-Boy announced.

They all left the scene before the state troopers and the local police arrived. On the way back, D-Boy announced an idea that John had given him in his earpiece.

"I got an idea. Let's get one of our new Lost Soul members to report to King Cobra that the Diaz brothers were killed in the battle. We can stage it to make it look like you are riddled with bullets to send a picture. This way, we can reverse it on them and make it look like you're out of the game," D-Boy said.

"That's another good idea. That will give us time to build a stronger army," Fernando replied.

"It will also give us time to ambush King Cobra because his communication line has been compromised, but he doesn't know it yet," D-Boy added from John's instructions.

"If I didn't know any better, I would've thought you were getting help from someone or something the way you're able to strategize," Fernando stated with curiosity.

"You can say that I have someone very powerful who knows some things on my side," D-Boy said, knowing that John could hear him.

John smiled. "You need to hurry up and stage that picture to send to King Cobra."

D-Boy entered the kitchen and saw some Frank's RedHot sauce. "We'll use this as fake blood." He started dosing Diego and Fernando with the hot sauce, making it seem as if they were bloody and lying there dead.

The two former Lost Soul soldiers, Juan and Henry, stood while José took the picture. D-Boy and the Diaz brothers looked at the pictures until they were all satisfied with the look they were trying to achieve.

"Damn, I never looked this dead in my life," Fernando said while viewing the photos.

Diego laughed. "I know. I'm not trying to end up like this in real life."

"Now you can send it to King Cobra," D-Boy told Juan.

KING COBRA'S UNDERGROUND COMPOUND

Rodolfo got a phone call from Juan. "It's done. We killed the Diaz brothers." Juan paused. "I'm sending over some pictures as proof."

Rodolfo looked at the pictures of Fernando and Diego covered with blood and smiled. "Good fucking job, Juan. King Cobra will be very pleased with you for carrying out his orders." Rodolfo hung up the phone and rushed to show

King Cobra. "King Cobra, sir, I have something to show you."

King Cobra stood by his side to view the pictures of the Diaz brothers lying there dead. "That's what you get for fucking with the King!" he shouted. "Now, let's get to America, where we can take over the Diaz brothers' operation and fuse it with the Lost Souls Cartel. No one can stop us now."

"Yes, sir," Rodolfo answered as he quickly made calls to prepare for the trip to the U.S.

THE WARLORD. SANDY SPRINGS, GEORGIA

John sat in the Warlord, listening to Rodolfo and King Cobra's conversation. He thought about his next move. Now that it was confirmed that they fell for the bait, John's plans were easy to execute.

"They fell for it hook, line, and sinker. The element of intelligence and surprise is on our side," John told D-Boy.

"We need the element of intelligence and surprise on our side when it comes to Agent Heron, and this whole game is over," D-Boy replied.

"We would have them if he hadn't taken Grandpa Joe, which, strangely, I'm glad that he kidnapped Grandpa Joe."

"You're glad that they took him?" D-Boy was confused. "What could be good about this sadistic bastard taking my grandfather?"

"Before Heron kidnapped Grandpa Joe, I had no idea where he was operating from. Now, I have the exact location of his safe house, which gives us the upper hand to gather intel for a surprise, if that makes sense."

"Yeah, but I wish Grandpa Joe wasn't a part of this. He's too old to be going through this shit." D-Boy felt sorry for his grandpa.

"He's tough; besides, if I were Heron, I would treat him like an honored guest. He knows if he tortures him, he'll have no leverage to use him as a bargaining chip," John stated.

"Let's hope you're right." D-Boy stopped talking because Fernando was approaching him. "What good, Fernando?"

"What do you want to do with the girl?" Fernando wanted to kill her.

D-Boy thought for a second. "She's still useful just in case King Cobra keeps his word and sends her the reward money. We could use it and keep her around to do jobs for the cartel."

"You trust her?"

"No, but I know we need more soldiers, male *and* female."

"You're right about that. I was just checking." Fernando paused and gave D-Boy a serious look. "Just so you know, she's your responsibility. If it were up to me, I would put a bullet in her head."

"I got you." D-Boy gave him a handshake to seal the deal, then walked to his room to check on her.

He found her sitting in the same spot, tied to the bedpost, when he opened the door. "Can you please untie me so I can use the bathroom?" Dalia pleaded.

D-Boy untied her and escorted her to the bathroom.

When she was done, he instructed her to sit on her hands again. He didn't trust her, but there was something about her that he liked. Maybe it was his 180-degree turn from the game, or he was falling for her. Whatever it was, he didn't want her dead. Although his intuition was telling him to let Fernando kill her, he wanted to see her live and change her life for the better, as he did.

In those seven years he spent away from his friends and family, D-Boy grew tremendously under John's tutelage. John introduced D-Boy to spirituality and many other sciences that assisted in elevating his consciousness. He saw the error in his ways and vowed to live his life fixing problems instead of being one.

"You know that making me sit on my hands isn't necessary. I'm not going to do anything," Dalia said in a tone so sweet that it was relaxing.

"All right, but any funny moves and you're dead." He gave her the look of death.

"Trust me, I'm only 25. I'm trying to live a long life," she spoke humbly.

D-Boy looked at her as if he were examining her through a microscope. She was aesthetically pleasing to his eye. Her skin was the color of golden wheat, and her chestnut-hazel eyes were the shape of a doe's eyes. Her face was oval shaped with high cheekbones, and she had a small nose and full lips that opened up to pearly straight teeth that formed a beautiful smile. Her hair was autumn brown. It fell in natural curly layers just beyond her shoulders. Her breasts were plump, and so was her backside. She seemed flawless.

"Why are you looking at me like that? Is there something wrong?" She knew her power over men, so the question was rhetorical. The look in his eyes told it all.

"Where do you come from, like what part of the world? Your ethnicity." D-Boy was never a man without words, but now, he was bewildered.

"I was born in Marrakech, Morocco. My mother is from there, and my father is a Black man from America, born and raised in Atlanta, Georgia. He was stationed in Marrakech in the marines, and that's how they met and made me. He left before I was born." She liked D-Boy, so she opened up to him by showing him the woman she really was.

"You look like a nice girl. I've been in the streets, so I can tell you're not cut from that cloth." He paused. "How the fuck did you get yourself caught up in this shit with the cartels?"

"That's the thing. I didn't know this had anything to do with a cartel." She took a deep breath to compose herself. "When I moved to Atlanta to stay with my father, I got involved with these rich girls from Buckhead who put me on to Nitro. One of them got the text message and shared it with me. I had no idea that the Diaz brothers were a cartel or that the text came from a cartel. When I saw that the pics matched the two guys standing in front of me, I made the call. I was just thinking about the $100K. I didn't know it was going to end with me almost getting killed." Dalia had tears in her eyes.

D-Boy put his arm around her and dried her tears with his hand. "It's going to be OK. People make mistakes. The thing is to bounce back and learn from them. You're right. They almost killed you. These are dangerous men you're involved with." He looked her in the eyes. "But I got you. I'm not going to let anything happen to you."

"You promise?" the little girl in her came out. "Because I trust you, D-Boy." She kissed his lips.

"My word is my bond." He kissed her back

He thought back to their episode of having sex, and his manhood began to rise. She was getting moist. They kissed each other and grinded. The chemistry between them was perfect. They were physically attracted to each other, and after the conversation, they were emotionally attracted as well.

He put his hand on her left breast and squeezed it before taking it out to suck the nipple. Then his phone rang. "Fuck. I have to take this call." He stood up and moved toward the far side of the room to speak. "What do you want?"

"That's no way to talk to the man who holds your life in his hands." Heron smiled.

"Enough of the games. What do you want?" D-Boy was frustrated that he had to deal with him.

"I need you to come in for the day and to see your grandfather. You can hear him in the background."

"Dammit! I want to see my grandson. Fuck this shit. Y'all got me locked in this damn room, and I want to see D-Boy," Grandpa Joe yelled at the top of his lungs.

"Your ride is pulling up to the Diaz mansion in two minutes. Be outside and ready." Heron turned to Grandpa Joe. "Now, you can shut the fuck up."

Grandpa Joe obliged and quietly changed the channel on his TV.

D-Boy put on his shoes and jacket, ready to meet his ride.

"Where are you going?" Dalia asked in a seductive tone. "Let me finish what we started."

"I can't. I have to go see my grandfather." He grabbed her face in both hands and kissed her passionately. "I'll be back." D-Boy headed for the door.

Dalia crossed her arms and pouted her full lips as she watched him exit the room.

CHAPTER 8
SOUND MASTERS STUDIO.
LONG ISLAND, NEW YORK

DIRTY REDD and Mouf were back at it in the studio to record their first album without Prime. Prime was a big part of the creative force contributing to the group's success. Without him, they were feeling the loss. It was like a soldier returning home without his legs. The Billigoats would never be the same without Prime.

"This shit feels weird without the god Prime here, adding to the cypher." Mouf spoke in a melancholy tone.

"It's like, I know he wants us to keep going, but it just doesn't feel like the Billigoats without Prime. I kind of don't even want to do this shit no more," Dirty Redd responded in the same tone.

"Like you said, Prime would want us to keep going in his name," Mouf said.

"You right."

Mouf looked at his phone and saw a notification on social media. He rolled his eyes and shook his head. "All day, I've been getting notifications about YC having the number one spot on the Billboard for four months straight. We have to start cooking or get cooked." Mouf's competitive nature was kicking in.

"Fuck it, let's cook!" Dirty Redd shouted.

"This one's for you, Prime."

The engineer pulling up the beat diverted their attention from the conversation. The song was about their fallen comrade, Prime. It was one of the hardest songs the two of them ever had to record. Mouf had to stop twice because the tears wouldn't stop falling. Dirty Redd had the same issue when it was his turn. It took them some time, but they finally got through it. When they finished, they sat down to listen to it and felt relief.

"Man, that was the hardest verse I ever had to spit, but now that I'm listening to it, it feels like therapy. I needed to get that off my chest," Mouf professed after listening to the song three times in a row.

"You right! Now that I'm listening to it, I feel calm. The way you feel after crying, then you feel peace afterward," Dirty Redd concurred.

"I'm not going to front," the engineer interjected. "This is one of the best dedications to a dead homie I've ever heard."

Mouf and Dirty Redd both gave him a handshake for his comment.

"Good looking, my G," Mouf said.

"Word. I know you got good judgment. I appreciate it," Dirty Redd concurred.

"What're you getting into tonight? I'm performing at S.O. B.'s. Come through and perform one of our old joints together. I'll throw you $5,000 for five minutes," Mouf proposed.

"I would've did it for nothing, but I have a new mortgage, so I'll be there. Send me the info." Dirty Redd gave him a sly grin.

Mouf laughed. "All right, my G. I'll see you at S.O.B.'s. I go on at 11:00 p.m." Mouf gave Dirty Redd a handshake before exiting the studio.

Dirty Redd's notification from his social media inbox was blowing up. He looked at the messages. "You are so handsome! I wish I could just see you again."

A picture was attached to the text, but he didn't recognize the face or the name. Jennifer Perkins. But she was very appealing to him. He smiled and responded, "You're not too bad yourself." He paused. "Where did we meet?"

"I met you at a meet and greet in Connecticut. We took a picture." As she said that, she sent over another picture of them at a concert meet and greet.

"Wow, I remember that concert."

"I'll never forget it. Maybe one day I'll see you again."

"I would love that. Where you at?" Dirty Redd asked.

"I moved to Atlanta, but I would go to the edge of the earth to be with you."

"That's funny. My homie just went down there on some business. I was thinking about visiting. Maybe we could set up something when I come down there," he suggested.

"I would love that. Just let me know when you're here."

"That's a bet. I'll talk to you later." Dirty Redd ended the text conversation.

He viewed the pictures posted on her social media page.

"She's just my type, exotic with a nice body and a pretty face. I could use a new shorty to play with. I haven't fucked since I left Dubai, and Sarah disappeared on me." He stopped scrolling when he saw a sexy picture of her in a bikini. *I'm about to tear that ass up when I see you*, he thought as he entertained the notion of hooking up with this new woman.

Sarah smiled from ear to ear.

That was easier than I thought, well, easier than the first time. Although this girl is pretty, she's not me. However, she got the job done.

Sarah looked at the fake social media profile she had created to bait Dirty Redd. She found a fan who had a picture posted on social media of her and Dirty Redd at a concert. It even had the date and the arena where they took the photo. Sarah used all that information to fool Dirty Redd into believing this girl was real.

Sarah smiled. "He fell for it hook, line, and sinker." She folded her laptop and lay down her pregnant stomach, ready to rest. Before she dozed off, she played the Billigoats' album and inserted her AirPods.

She daydreamed about making love to Dirty Redd while she listened to his verse in a song. She didn't hear Heron stroll into the room. He was admiring her with her eyes closed.

Look at my sleeping beauty. I hope she's having a boy. George Cletus Heron the Third.

He stood over her to kiss her, but Sarah opened her eyes right before his lips landed on her forehead. When she saw it was Heron disturbing her fantasy about Dirty Redd, she couldn't hide the disgust that ran through her body. She rolled her eyes at him, pushed him to the side, and got up.

"I was just getting some rest not even 15 minutes, and here you come!" she lashed out.

"I'm sorry, sweetheart. I couldn't resist getting a kiss. You looked so peaceful."

"That's the magic word: peaceful." She waltzed into the living room to lie on the couch where she could finish her daydream about her true love, Dirty Redd.

Heron stood there with his jaw on the floor from Sarah's reaction to his romantic attempt.

"She has never acted like that with me. Maybe the pregnancy is making her cranky," he thought.

A phone call snapped him back to reality. "Director Cohen, what do I owe the pleasure?" Heron knew whenever Director Cohen called, it was mandatory that you answer the call.

"I'm completely hands-off. You're on your own with this one from here on out, which means if you're compromised, I know nothing, and we never worked together on it. In fact, you should think about dropping this whole D-Boy thing before it bites you in the ass," Director Cohen spoke directly and to the point.

"Why the sudden change? I thought the $10 million I just wired you would make you a happy camper."

"With Trump back in office, they are investigating all the agencies' activities. They will go through our records with a fine-tooth comb." Director Cohen spoke like his life was on the line.

"Let them look. Our operation is ironclad. There's no way for them to discover anything because our hands are clean. But I understand your caution. However, I assure you we're safe from anyone's investigation." Heron closed his eyes in anticipation of Cohen's response.

Director Cohen paused. "OK, but I'm giving you six months, and then I'm shutting it down myself. Understood?"

"Yes, Director Cohen, sir."

"Good." Director Cohen ended the call.

Agent Heron had to process the conversation with Director Cohen. Six months wasn't enough time for him to achieve his goal. He was trying to make a billion dollars from his cartel involvement. He knew it was possible because he was doing business with the Diaz brothers. They were moving product faster than any cartel in history. Cohen thought five years with the Diaz brothers would get him to his billion-dollar goal.

"Sorry, Director Cohen, but I have other plans." Heron let the power of making millions of dollars go to his head.

He knew that disobeying Cohen would mean certain death. He also knew that Cohen had more to lose than he did because of his rank in the Agency. He would be faced with treason, which is punishable by death. That equaled the playing field for Heron. It also made it dangerous to leave the director alive. It was a far-fetched idea but one that Heron was willing to entertain.

"I'm going to get you first, Director Cohen. Checkmate." Heron lit a cigar and sat back in his expensive office chair.

Heron didn't see it, but greed and corruption were getting the better part of him. Once a man becomes corrupt absolutely, he is absolutely corrupt. There was no turning back for Heron. Once he got the taste of his first $10 million, the hunger for more became ferocious. He made his first $10 mil the first year he started the operation 10 years ago with D-Boy and Jay-Roc.

Since that day, Heron has recruited 20 more D-Boys to sell drugs for him. The dealers he recruited usually didn't last long; they didn't have the same business savvy as the original D-Boy. They got locked up, and Heron couldn't help them because he didn't want the connection made to the CIA, or they were robbed and killed by rival dealers. He only had five left, and his number one guy was YC.

Heron walked to the section of the house that held Grandpa Joe. He was met with D-Boy and Grandpa Joe when he unlocked the door. D-Boy was visiting. His job was to be the liaison between Heron and the Diaz brothers since they killed Haitian John. His visits with Grandpa Joe were limited.

When Heron entered the room, D-Boy's face went from joy to irritation in a split second. He truly despised Heron; he had daily visions of killing him with his bare hands. D-Boy knew there was no way out because Heron had the code to exit the house. And the road leading to the house was lined with explosives that had to be deactivated before driving on it.

"Why the long face, D-Boy? Are you sad because it's time to say bye-bye to Grandpa Joe?" Heron knew how to get under his skin.

If I could kill Heron and get Grandpa Joe out of the safe house alive, he'd be dead already, D-Boy thought.

D-Boy pretended like Heron wasn't there. He stood and walked over to his grandfather. "I'll see you soon. I love you, Grandpa Joe." He hugged him.

"I love you too, D-Boy."

"I'm sorry I got you into this mess, but I promise to make it up to you." D-Boy let him go and walked out of the room with Heron.

Agent J was sitting in the driver's seat of the Mercedes waiting for them. As soon as he saw them approach the car, he started the vehicle and unlocked the doors. D-Boy was very quiet and distant around Heron and Agent J. There was no need for him to pretend to like this situation. He wouldn't do this to his worst enemy, so his energy toward them was mutual.

I can't wait to watch both of you die slowly, he thought as they drove to the Diaz mansion.

When they arrived, D-Boy moved to exit the car, but Heron stopped him. "Listen, always remember that the moment you decide to try anything funny, I'm going to feed Grandpa Joe to Agent J. Trust me, it's not going to be nice. Capice?" Heron winked his eye.

"Is that all?" D-Boy asked cynically.

"For now."

D-Boy shook his head. *I can't wait*, he thought before slamming the car door and entering the mansion.

D-Boy was greeted by Fernando. "I need to talk to you." Fernando walked to his office for privacy.

"What's good, Fernando?" D-Boy was curious to hear what he had to say.

"We have to get rid of the girl. She's a loose end we don't need alive," he said sternly.

D-Boy was silent as he thought, *I'm not letting you kill Dalia. I'll kill you first. She's innocent.*

Fernando saw his hesitation in responding to his statement. He detected that D-Boy was opposed to killing her. He was waiting for him to answer so he would know what move to make. What D-Boy said would determine what happens to Dalia . . . and himself.

"I spoke to her about how she got mixed up in this mess. She's an innocent bystander who was with the wrong people and place at the wrong time." D-Boy gave Fernando a sincere look. "Let her live, Fernando. I'll keep her with me until my job here is done so you can be sure she's no threat to your organization."

Fernando thought about it before replying. "OK, I won't kill her. But if she does anything out of pocket, you will meet the same fate as her." Fernando looked at D-Boy dead in his eyes for clarity.

D-Boy stared back. "Understood." He stood up to leave the office.

"Oh yeah . . ." D-Boy stopped in his tracks and turned around to give Fernando his undivided attention. "I want to personally thank you for assisting us in the battle with King Cobra and the Lost Souls. Your strategy was impeccable, and I would like you to be the head of security. Starting pay is $12 million a year, which is a million a month."

"Let me think about it." D-Boy left the office and headed for his suite.

There's nothing for me to think about. I'm out of the game. No amount of money can get me back in, he thought as he walked.

When he got to his room, Dalia was resting. D-Boy took a moment to admire her beauty. *Damn, she is so beautiful*, he thought as he moved closer.

Right before he was within touching distance, Dalia

opened her eyes and smiled at seeing D-Boy. "I missed you," she said with a smile.

D-Boy kissed her on her forehead. "You hungry? I want to take you out for dinner. You've been couped up in this room for days now."

"I don't have a change of clothes or anything," she protested.

"I'll take you shopping before dinner. Put your shoes on, and let's go." They headed for the four-car garage. Fernando told him he could drive any one of the cars in the garage as a perk for working with the Diaz brothers. He looked at the four cars and chose a black-on-black Rolls-Royce Wraith. He saw the keys and opened the garage before getting in the car and starting it up.

Dalia sat in the passenger seat, and they headed out for their first date. D-Boy drove smoothly as they chatted more about family and life experiences. It was easy for them to open up to each other because they were both feeling the vibe. Dalia felt comfortable and safe, which was what attracted her to D-Boy even more.

"I've been in love twice and have had my heart broken twice. That's why I just date, and I don't have sex a lot unless I really like the guy. I knew I wanted you from the moment I laid eyes on you." She grabbed his right hand and held it tight. "Please don't hurt me, D-Boy. I really like you and know I just met you, but I—" She paused to find the right words. "I really like you, that's all." She turned her head toward the window and removed her hand from his.

D-Boy noticed the shift in her mood. "What just happened?"

"It always starts the same way, with me professing my

love for a man, and then he takes it for granted and breaks my heart. I'm afraid of getting hurt because I'm falling for you." She turned her head to look him in the eyes.

"I'm falling for you too, Dalia, and I promise I won't hurt you. Let's just enjoy each other's company and live stress-free lives." D-Boy smiled, which was rare for him, so when he did, it felt like a monumental occasion.

Dalia smiled back. "That sounds like a plan."

D-Boy got a call from John. "What's good?"

"I'm three cars behind you. There's a QT gas station half a mile up. Pull in and go to the men's room," John instructed before hanging up.

Dalia wondered who was on the phone, but she decided to mind her own business and just go with the flow. She had a feeling from the context of the conversation that it was confidential. She didn't want to nag him. If he wanted her to know something, he would tell her. She was going into this relationship with no excess baggage.

D-Boy pulled into the gas station and parked right beside John's Warlord. "I'm going to use the bathroom." He walked to the bathroom and looked for John, but he was nowhere in sight.

A guy with red hair and the biggest nose D-Boy had ever seen entered the bathroom. He couldn't help glancing at his nose. He almost laughed because the way his nose was so elongated was comical.

"You got a problem?" the guy asked D-Boy rudely.

"You talking to me?"

"Yeah, who else would I be talking to?" the guy responded.

"Listen, I don't want any problems, so I'm going to get

out of here before I fuck up your ass." D-Boy moved to exit the bathroom when the guy grabbed his arm.

"It's me," John said.

D-Boy had to think twice before speaking. "John?"

He winked his eye. "I had to brush up on my disguise skills. It's been a while since I tried out one of my disguises. I know it's a good one when I can fool you."

D-Boy laughed. "You had me because I kept thinking about your nose, how big it was. I couldn't stop looking at it."

"The nose is the most distinct part of the face, so that's what I concentrate on when designing a new disguise."

"That makes sense, but I know you didn't meet me here to test out your new disguise." D-Boy knew John too well.

John locked the door before speaking. "I did a background check on Dalia, and something came back."

"What do you mean something came back?" D-Boy's heart skipped a beat because he was just bonding with her.

"It's nothing criminal; however, it is something you need to know. I didn't want to spill the beans while you were in her presence," John replied.

"Man, get to it. What came up?" D-Boy was getting impatient.

John pointed his phone toward the wall, and a 3-D hologram of Dalia and her family appeared. As he spoke, the scenes changed with his narration. "Dalia is a fugitive from Marrakesh, but not for committing a crime. Apparently, she is the only child of Fatima Shahrah, the princess of Marrakesh. She has been missing from her people for a year and a half."

D-Boy took a deep breath. "I'm just glad it's nothing

crazy because I really like this woman. So, what's the bad side to this situation?"

"There is an international hunt for her because her grandfather, King Fayez of Marrakesh, just passed, so they need Dalia so she can be coronated to her new position as princess of Marrakesh. Her mother is now Queen Fatima of Marrakesh. Without Dalia, the structure of their nation is cracked, and the tradition of her people is upended," John explained.

D-Boy took a moment to inhale this information before responding. "So, what's the worst that can happen?"

"When they find her, they will take her into custody and fly her back home to be coronated, most likely against her will, so I expect kidnapping will be enacted. From my experience, they will try to kill anyone with her who's in the way. That means you," John said.

"So, basically, I have to watch our backs for woman-napping bandits from Marrakesh."

John nodded. "That sums it up in a nutshell. You know I got your back." He stopped the hologram and dapped D-Boy with his fist. "Stay alert. See you soon." He exited the bathroom.

D-Boy was shocked about Dalia's true identity. He wasn't even mad at her for withholding it. He actually found her more attractive now.

"My new shorty is the princess of Marrakesh. Who would've thought." D-Boy exited the gas station bathroom and got in the car.

"What took you so long? I was about to send in the search party looking for you," Dalia joked with him.

D-Boy laughed, not at her joke but at the thought.

Speaking of a search party, you have a whole nation searching for you.

He drove toward their destination to go shopping. He wanted to probe her to see if she would tell him the truth. He didn't want to reveal that he knew without giving her a chance to tell him on her own. It was a matter of principle to D-Boy. Honesty was paramount to him.

"Tell me a little more about your upbringing," he asked.

Dalia became nervous and uncomfortable. "Like what? What do you want to know?"

D-Boy detected her agitation. "Were you poor? Are you close to your grandparents? What were your parents like? I'm trying to get to know you, the *real* you. I'm really big on honesty. Once I feel you can't be truthful, all bets are off." He gave her a serious look.

She locked eye contact with him and saw his stare was intense. Thoughts were racing through her mind. *I like him so much. What if he finds out the truth without me telling him? It's not the worst thing to tell someone you're a fugitive from your life as a royal. I have to follow my heart.*

He watched her contemplate her next move. She took a deep breath and closed her eyes, something she often did in nerve-racking times like this. She bit her lip, blinked, and took another deep breath.

"My mother is Princess Fatima Shahrah of the Republic of Marrakesh, Morrocco. My whole life I was told that my father died in a car accident until two years ago when my mother told me the truth. My mother fell in love with Erick Johnson, a sergeant in the United States Marines stationed in Marrakesh. When her father, my grandfather King Fayez, found out, he was opposed to their relationship because Erick was a black man. King Fayez denounced her unless she rejected Erick. Since my grandfather didn't have a son to ascend his throne, my mother's husband would become the new king of Marrakesh once Papa died. When I learned the truth, I left Marrakesh searching for my real father in Atlanta." Dalia let out a sigh of relief.

"Wow! You're joking, right? I'm waiting for you to say, 'Got ya!'" He played the part of the surprised boyfriend well.

"I'm not joking, so you can stop waiting. I'm really heir to the Kingdom of Marrakesh," she smirked.

D-Boy had to pretend he was processing this information for the first time.

"If you're not there to rule, wouldn't they look for you? Something like sending a search party," he alluded to the joke she told earlier.

"Yeah, they're looking for me. That's why I've been living life under the radar. I'm still on the grid but under different names."

"I'm still trying to take all this in." He paused. "I'm glad you told me. This way, I can help you. If I didn't know, we would be out here moving around like nothing was wrong." He grabbed her hand and kissed it. "I got you, baby. You're safe with me."

She hugged him tightly. "Thank you, D-Boy. I'm so happy that the Creator brought you into my life." She kissed his face passionately.

"Now that we got that out of the way, I'm taking you shopping and then out to eat." He kissed her lips and drove straight to Lenox Mall.

D-Boy spared no expense on his new woman. He still

had millions left from being in the game. He didn't have to work another day in his life. He had enough money to last him for the rest of his life. They waltzed through the designer section of the mall, buying expensive items from several high-end stores. He ended up spending $10,000 in the Gucci and Fendi stores alone, not counting Louis Vuitton and the MCM stores. D-Boy spent a whopping $35,000 shopping for Dalia.

Then they went across the street to Meso-America to eat the best Mexican cuisine on earth. That whole time, they talked about past relationships and life in general. They were quickly forming a strong bond.

"That food was amazing," Dalia professed.

"The first time I came to Atlanta, I ate here and said the same thing. I'm glad you liked it."

"I'm ready to go home and give you some dessert." She gave him a seductive smile.

"I can't wait to taste you." They kissed like all lovers do.

THE BAR AT THE MESO-AMERICAN RESTAURANT

The bartender kept staring at Dalia. She was someone important, but he couldn't put his finger on it. Hakeem was a newly transplanted immigrant from Marrakesh in America on a six-month visa. Before he left Marrakesh, all the citizens talked about was the disappearance of Princess Dalia.

He pulled out his phone and secretly filmed the two lovebirds kissing. When they unlocked, he took snapshots of Dalia. He compared them to the pictures of the princess of Marrakesh. It was a match.

There was a hotline to call if anyone spotted her. "Yes, my name is Hakeem Ibn Abdul, and I'm looking at the princess of Marrakesh right now."

"Can you FaceTime us to confirm?"

Hakeem put his phone in FaceTime mode and recorded Dalia. "That's her! Send us the location ASAP!"

Hakeem shared his location, and they were able to contact one of their bounty hunters in Atlanta. The bounty hunter was in the area, so he was there within minutes. He parked facing the exit of the establishment so he would see them coming out.

"Thank you for your service, Hakeem. The queen will reward you and your family handsomely."

"Thank you so much." The call ended, and Hakeem went back to work.

D-BOY WAS STARTING to feel the effects of the drinks. So was Dalia. They enjoyed each other, and time flew by quickly because they were having fun. This was something that D-Boy needed in his life. After seven years on the run, he was ready to settle down and have a family. He loved the way Jay-Roc was raising his nephew, little D-Boy. He wanted a little D-Boy of his own, and Dalia was the perfect candidate to be his wife.

"I'm ready to go home now," Dalia slurred.

"Let me get the check," D-Boy said to their server.

He paid the check, and they both stumbled to the car. The bounty hunter watched as they got into the Rolls-

Royce and drove off. Then he followed them at a distance to the Diaz mansion, where he couldn't enter because of the heavy iron gate. He drove past the house, parked on the street, and made a call.

"Greetings, Queen Fatima. I'm at the exact location of your daughter, Princess Dalia."

"Is she safe? Is the house rundown? Can you get her out of there and bring her back to Marrakesh?" The queen has been worried sick about the disappearance of her only daughter.

"Oh, she's safe, all right. She's living in a mansion built like a fortress. She was driving in a $250,000 Rolls-Royce, and I doubt I can just waltz in there and take her with me. We might need to call in some reinforcements," the bounty hunter informed her.

The queen smiled. "I have the perfect man for the job. Thank you for your services. Your job is done once you send me her location. Your money will be wired to your account as promised." She ended the call and made another one.

"Your Majesty Queen Fatima, what do I owe the honor of speaking to you?"

"Remember you said you owed me a favor?" she asked.

"Yes, I do."

"Well, I need it." She paused to text him the address of the Diaz brothers' mansion. "My daughter is at this location. It's heavily guarded, but I need her secretly extracted and returned to me in Marrakesh unharmed."

"Not a problem. I'll have my people on it ASAP." Director Cohen ended the call.

He hesitated but knew Heron was the only one he could call for this type of covert dirty work.

"I really hate doing anything with this asshole Heron," Director Cohen said to himself before calling.

"Director Cohen, twice in a couple of days I'm feeling special," Heron said playfully.

"I need an extraction, but it has to be super covert, and no harm can come to the asset."

"I'll assemble a team. Just send over the intel, and I'll have the asset within 48 hours."

"Copy." Cohen ended the call and sent the address and a picture of Dalia.

When Heron saw the picture, he didn't recognize Dalia, but when he read the address, he cocked his head to the side. "I've seen this address before." He kept thinking until he remembered. "Well, I'll be a monkey's uncle. That's the address of the Diaz brothers' mansion. Why would the Diaz brothers be harboring a missing princess from Marrakesh?" He lit up a cigar. "This is going to be fun." He smiled as he let out a thick cloud of smoke.

CHAPTER 9
YC'S MANSION IN ALPHARETTA, GEORGIA

YC's mansion was like a 24-hour, seven-days-a-week house party. You could always find a dozen gorgeous women, a few homies, some weed, and plenty of drinks with loud music pumping. That was how he liked to live, the "lit life," as he called it. He was getting so much paper that he could afford it and not skip a beat. YC was the new king of Atlanta.

"Stuck 'em!" Scoop yelled. "I told you me and YC can't be fucked with in a game of Spades."

"We been partners in Spades since doing time in juvie," YC added.

A thick, red-bone girl came and sat on YC's lap. She was smoking a blunt that she passed to him. He took two healthy pulls and handed it back to her. She took the blunt and walked back to the group of people standing in the living room.

"Who got next on the Spades game?" Scoop asked while removing himself and tapping YC on the shoulder.

"Hey, let me holla at you in private." Scoop moved to an empty room.

YC followed him, knowing what the conversation would be about none other than Nitro. He entered the room and closed the door. "What's up, my boy?" he asked.

"You know what's up. I need like 10 bricks of Nitro for my people in Columbus and Macon. I'm running through 10 in three days. Your people need to get more of that shit in. I really need 20, but I'm holding off to pay my house off."

"I feel you, my boy. I'm supposed to be getting another ton shipped in, but the shit is taking too long. Let me holla at my people, and I'll get back to you."

"Copy that." Scoop left the room so YC could call Fernando.

Fernando was sitting in the steam room when YC called. "What' s up, my brother? I already know what you're going to say. It's coming."

"So when can I let my folks know when to expect it? They are hounding me like crackheads about this shit."

"They said it'll be here today or tomorrow. That's all I can tell you." Fernando summoned a woman to come over and massage him.

"What's up with D-Boy? Is he still fucking with that ho from the party?" YC asked.

"Yeah, he's been with her daily for the last two weeks. I told him we should've killed the bitch because she tried to set us up. But he said she was innocent and didn't know who she was working with, blah, blah, blah." Fernando was annoyed even talking about the situation.

"I feel you. It ain't like she's the last fine ho in Atlanta.

I'm going to talk to him about that shit because he going out bad."

Fernando switched the subject. "We're taking care of that snake King Cobra this week. He's not going to see this shit coming." He smiled.

"Then we're going to have another celebration, only this time not at your mansion." YC slightly chuckled at his comment.

"Facts," Fernando concurred.

BUCKHEAD SECTION OF ATLANTA, GEORGIA

King Cobra easily crossed the southern border with Rodolfo and four soldiers. He rented a beautiful six-bedroom estate in the ritzy Buckhead area about 10 minutes from Phipps Plaza. He planned to take over the U.S. market now that the Diaz brothers were out of the way . . . or so he thought.

The three Lost Souls, now devoted Diaz Brothers' Cartel soldiers, were feeding King Cobra false information. They told him the market was wide open for him to take control of. No one has been able to purchase Nitro because the Diaz brothers were the only ones who knew the secret ingredient making it so potent. He had no reason not to believe them. Besides, they were trusted and loyal soldiers of the Lost Souls Cartel. However, he would soon discover that the Diaz brothers were alive and well.

There was a double entendre of events taking place: King Cobra thought the Diaz brothers were dead, and Heron thought King Cobra was dead. This was working out better for King Cobra because the CIA is the wrong agency to want you dead. He figured he could get around a newly formed cartel of a few dozen members. King Cobra was about to make the mistake of underestimating the underdog and the element of surprise.

"Everything is all set. We meet with the three surviving Lost Souls tomorrow," Rodolfo informed King Cobra.

"Good. They've been supplying the Diaz brothers' customers with our product as instructed?"

"Yes, sir. They have been successful at taking control of the Diaz brothers' leftover territory."

"What do you mean, 'leftover territory'? Is there territory that isn't leftover?" King Cobra asked, confused.

"Well, the Diaz brothers had some soldiers still holding down most of the area they controlled. Our men couldn't take over everything at once, but they will." Rodolfo knew that wasn't acceptable.

"I want it all or nothing!" King Cobra slammed his fist on the table, causing Rodolfo and the other men in the room to jump. "We are the Lost Souls Cartel! We don't stop until we got it all!" King Cobra was known for throwing these types of childish fits, so Rodolfo learned to stay quiet while he was ranting.

After an hour of King Cobra letting off some steam, he retired to his room with two women. Rodolfo was relieved of his duties of catering to King Cobra's ego, which was like taming a dragon. It was impossible to get King Cobra to be humble. He was always in a state of anxiety and attack. There was never a moment of peace with him. It was constant aggression all day, every day.

Rodolfo closed his eyes and sighed. *About time this man took a break from his constant tirade. I need a break from him. I'm losing myself. I don't even know who I am anymore.* He often thought about killing him. *Life would be better without King Cobra living. I genuinely hate that man and everything he stands for. That's why most of his soldiers jumped ship on him in the first place.*

Rodolfo often thought like this when he was alone. He really couldn't stand King Cobra's guts, and he wanted to kill him on many occasions. The only thing that was stopping him was the other soldiers around him. They were indoctrinated to fear him to the point that they would rather commit suicide than even think about taking out their boss.

When Rodolfo started his life as a Lost Soul, he dedicated his entire being to the organization. He rose to the rank of captain in no time after King Cobra murdered Captain Diaz for his association with his nephews, the Diaz brothers. All the soldiers revered the tough old Captain Diaz. He was a throwback to the days of real men. King Cobra made a big mistake when he killed him. It was the start of the end for him, but he didn't even know it. His ego blinded him.

I can't wait for the day . . . Rodolfo dozed off with thoughts of King Cobra dead running through his head.

THE DIAZ BROTHERS' MANSION

D-Boy couldn't keep his hands off Dalia and vice versa. They were making love several times a day like clockwork. They were enjoying each other so much that when one went to the bathroom, they practically suffered from separation anxiety. D-Boy and Dalia had never experienced a love connection like this before. It was very intense for both of them.

"Would you be open to moving with me to Marrakesh?" Dalia asked him while resting her head on his chest.

"Of course. I lived in Dubai for seven years. I love Middle Eastern culture," D-Boy responded.

"Marrakesh is a lot different from Dubai, but I get why people equate the two since we're both Islamic countries," she explained.

They were interrupted by a knock on the door. "Who is it?" D-Boy asked while getting up and putting on his clothes.

"It's your boy YC. I want to holla at you for a minute."

D-Boy exited the room and walked with YC to a remote corner of the mansion. D-Boy tried to stay clear of YC since he discovered they were cousins. He wanted to get to know YC as family, but right now, he couldn't. He had to stick to the mission or risk Grandpa Joe's life.

"What's good?" D-Boy gave YC a handshake.

"I just wanted to give you a heads-up. Niggas are looking at you crazy for making that ho from the party your wifey. I consider you like my . . ." he hesitated from saying family although he knew deep inside they were despite D-Boy denying it, "my people. You know what I'm saying?"

D-Boy knew the truth about Dalia, so what YC said had no merit. "I can understand what you're saying, but it's not what you think. One day, it'll all make sense, cuzo." D-Boy tapped him on the shoulder before walking back to the room.

Cuzo? This nigga trying to say we cousins while saying we not? YC thought to himself, bemused.

D-Boy entered the room and sat on the bed. Dalia lay there observing him in deep thought. He had to play it cool with YC because he didn't want to throw him in the mix, even though he was already knee-deep in it with the Diaz brothers. He wanted to save YC from his involvement with the Diaz brothers. D-Boy knew that Heron was using YC the same way he was using him when he was in the game. For now, he had to save Grandpa Joe. Then he could help YC.

"Is everything all right?" Dalia asked.

"Yeah, everything's fine."

D-Boy's phone rang. When he saw it was Heron, he took a deep breath before answering. "What's up?" he got up and went to the bathroom so Dalia couldn't hear the conversation.

"There's a woman there in the mansion, a Dalia Shahrah," Heron said.

"What about her?" D-Boy answered offensively.

"Surrender her to me, or I'll have to raid the house to take her by force."

D-Boy couldn't believe what he was hearing. The new love of his life was being taken away from him. He remained silent, thinking about Heron's command. The silence was loud because Heron sensed a connection between D-Boy and Dalia. The simple fact that D-Boy was asking questions and being silent told it all.

"Let me find out that D-Boy is sweet on the princess . . ." Heron assumed that D-Boy knew that Dalia was a runaway princess, and he was right.

"She's not going anywhere with you, so you might as well send in the squad."

"On the contrary, my friend, she will be coming with me, or you'll be going to Grandpa Joe's funeral. You got me?" Heron knew he had D-Boy in check by using Grandpa Joe as leverage.

D-Boy shook his head. He knew Heron had him in a tough position. He loved Dalia, but he couldn't risk getting his grandfather killed. He had to decide, and fast, but he had to contact John before making a choice. He knew John would have a strategic plan to save Grandpa Joe and Dalia.

"Give me a last day with her, and you can come get her tomorrow," D-Boy agreed.

"Good boy. I'll see you tomorrow at 12 noon sharp." Heron ended the call.

D-Boy stood in the bathroom, staring at himself in the mirror. He shook his head because the image he saw was the cause of everything. He blamed himself for everything bad that was happening—Grandpa Joe getting kidnapped, Dalia getting taken away—everything that was happening be blamed himself for. He was spiraling.

When he left the bathroom, Dalia was standing there. She had eavesdropped on his whole conversation. She heard enough to know that he was selling her out to Heron. She heard him loud and clear when he said, *"Give me a last day with her, and you can come get her tomorrow."*

"How could you do this to me?" Dalia asked with tears running down her face. "I trusted you with everything." She ran and threw herself on the bed and cried into the pillow.

D-Boy went after her and held her tightly. "It's not what you think."

"Then what is it? You told someone, 'She's not going

anywhere with you.' Then you told him to come get me after you spend one more day with me. Are you serious? One more day with me and whoever can come take me? That's how you *really* feel, D-Boy?"

D-Boy made a choice. He had to tell Dalia everything. He knew that was the only way for her to understand what was happening. He knew that John would oppose him telling her the truth about everything, but his heart was telling him otherwise. He felt like he had to do the right thing for his love.

She saw him contemplating. "Well, what do you have to say?"

D-Boy looked into her eyes. "There's a lot about me that I need to tell you." He paused to make sure he had her total attention before continuing. "My real name is Darius Jensen. Eight years ago, I faked my death, and that's why I lived in Dubai for seven years. Some rogue agents from the CIA were setting me up as the biggest heroin dealer on the East Coast. My lawyer and I found out about the plot, so we beat them to the punch, and we both faked our deaths to escape a real death or a possible lifetime prison sentence."

Dalia couldn't believe what she was hearing. It sounded like something out of a spy movie to her. "So, you're telling me that to the rest of the world, you're dead, and the guy on the phone, who was that?"

"That was Agent Heron from the CIA. He found out about us faking our deaths and kidnapped my grandfather to get me back into the drug game working for him. I vowed never to sell drugs again, but Heron is doing this to get back at us for outsmarting him."

"But I don't get it. How did the CIA find out that I was here?" Dalia asked.

"Good question. They have their hands in a lot of the world's affairs. Maybe they have some ties with your government. Who knows the real reason. All I know is that he called me asking me to surrender you to them, and I pretended to agree. I needed time to get with John so we could plan. That's what you heard. I was stalling to come up with a plan. I would never give you up. I love you." That was the first time D-Boy said those words to her.

"I love you too." She hugged him tightly.

"That's my word to God. I would never let anything happen to you, Dalia. You have to trust me."

Dalia nodded. "OK, I trust you."

D-Boy called John. "We have a problem."

"Big or small?" John asked.

"Big." he hesitated. "Heron called, demanding that I hand over Dalia to him or he will raid the Diaz mansion to take her by force."

John was already on his supercomputer, which could hack every governmental data system in seconds. His software was assembling anomalies that would make sense for how Queen Fatima and the CIA were connected. It didn't take 10 seconds for his system to give him the most probable answers.

"The queen of Marrakesh has met with Director Cohen of the CIA several times in the past few years about becoming an ally in the region. She gave them $50 million in government subsidies to build a base for the CIA in Marrakesh." He looked at other data that could factor into the equation. "There's also a cobalt deal on the table worth billions that Gill Bates is negotiating with Marrakesh through the CIA. I could see Director Cohen using his attack dog Heron for this type of dirty covert work. It's like a favor for a favor."

"I'm not letting them take her. I gave her my word that I wouldn't let anything happen to her." D-Boy showed a rare side of himself. He was always in control, and now things were out of his hands.

"I don't know about this one, D-Boy. You might have to let her go. She has obligations to her country and her people that must be taken care of as a matter of tradition. You can still be with her, but for now, you must stay on course to save Grandpa Joe." John hated to be the bearer of bad news, but D-Boy knew he was right.

D-Boy closed his eyes to stop them from crying. "You're right. We have to rescue Grandpa Joe and then kill Heron." He abruptly ended the call with John.

Trying to save his true love could kill one his most beloved family members . . . Grandpa Joe. He knew he couldn't live with himself, knowing he chose a woman over saving his grandfather. There was no way around it. D-Boy had to surrender Dalia to Heron to save Grandpa Joe.

Dalia listened to the whole conversation. She knew what had to be done. She couldn't see risking D-Boy's family member for her selfish agenda. She wasn't going to prison; she was going back to her homeland to be crowned the princess of Marrakesh. The worst thing that was happening was that they had to part ways as soon as their lovers' flame got hot.

Dalia shed her tears as she tried to find the right words. "I understand what has to be done and why. I'm not mad at you. I am just so sad that we have to be apart." She kissed him gently. "I love you, D-Boy. This is the hardest thing I have ever had to do."

"Don't worry. I'll see you again, I promise." He kissed her forehead. "I love you more, Dalia." He couldn't hold back the tears as they streamed down his face. They cried together.

"At least we have one last night together." She tried to smile, but it didn't come out right, mixed with the taste of her salty tears. She wiped her face with the back of her hands.

"Let's enjoy what little time we have left."

D-Boy kissed her hard and handled her rough, something he hadn't done with her in their short span together. He picked her up, threw her on the bed, and stripped off his clothes. Then he pulled her pants off as she took off her top. He dove into her vagina face-first, lapping up her juice as if it were the best drink on earth. She closed her eyes and leaned her head back in ecstasy as he took over her mind, body, and soul.

When he finished, she returned the favor putting her mouth on him and taking him deep in her throat. She began to gag but didn't stop. She kept going until she felt her gag reflex giving up.

"Damn, ma," D-Boy yelled in total bliss.

He lay on top of her and quickly inserted his penis in her vagina like it was a lifeline. "Oh, yes, baby," she screamed out.

He thrust in and out of her hard, then harder and faster. "That feels so good up in there." He felt himself about to ejaculate, stopped, and tried to pull out his penis.

But Dalia wrapped her legs around his back in a death grip, stopping him from pulling out. "No, don't take it out this time. Come inside me," she yelled while begging him with her eyes to grant her this wish. "Please."

D-Boy looked at her as if she were the most beautiful creature alive. "Yes, baby." He continued to pump into her until he felt the eruption explode inside her. "I'm coming!" he yelled out. He pushed himself as deep as he could to spray the back of her uterus with his cum.

"Oh my God, baby, yes."

D-Boy fell to the side, drained of energy. He just lay there taking deep breaths. Dalia was breathing erratically, trying to compose herself. The intermixing of bodily fluids created an emotional bond, one that would be strong. They were going down a road with bumps and cracks, but you still travel it, knowing that the adventure of love is worth the ride.

"I never before felt this connected to a man, and now, I have to go back to Marrakesh." Dalia cried again and buried her face in D-Boy's chest. "I wish I could stay here like this with you forever."

"We will not talk about you returning to Marrakesh tonight. All I want to do is create dope memories we won't forget." He turned her around and kissed her ravishingly.

His manhood became erect again, so he inserted it back into her. "Ready for round two?"

She welcomed him back into her while looking directly into his eyes. "I love you, D-Boy."

He responded by thrusting himself into her before saying, "I love you too."

They made love until the sun rose. Then they fell into a

deep sleep. They slept like babies, oblivious to anything in the physical realm, a place where time doesn't exist. It felt as though the five hours they slept were only five minutes. They were so knocked out from the night of lovemaking that they didn't hear Heron calling them.

D-Boy slowly opened his eyes because of the sound of his phone going off. He looked at the clock. It was 12:30 p.m. "Oh shit!" he got up, and Dalia's head fell off his chest, causing her to wake up abruptly.

"What happened?" she mumbled incoherently.

"They're here to take you back to Marrakesh." D-Boy quickly dressed.

"Damn. Can't they give us another week?" she asked sarcastically.

D-Boy answered the phone. "My bad. I was knocked out."

"For a second, I thought you were trying to renege on our agreement. But then I thought, D-Boy wouldn't get Grandpa Joe slaughtered over some pussy." Heron liked to make D-Boy panic from the threat of killing his grandfather. "Now, get your fucking sand nigger bitch to the fucking car before I personally cut off one of Grandpa Joe's fingers as a penalty." Heron hung up and lit a cigar.

D-Boy looked at the phone and shook his head. "One day," he muttered. "Get dressed. The car is here to take you to the airport." He suddenly turned cold. He had to protect his emotions for the mission.

Never let your emotions supersede your intelligence. D-Boy remembered John always telling him that.

Dalia noticed the sudden change in his demeanor. "Can you at least ride with me to the jet?"

"Yeah, I can do that, but we have to go now," he urgently commanded.

Dalia didn't say a word. She quickly packed the new clothes that D-Boy brought her. They walked past Fernando's office. Fernando knew the car was waiting for them. He wanted to know what was going on. He always inquired because it came with the territory.

"D-Boy, can I speak to you in my office?" Fernando asked. When he entered the office, Fernando glanced at Dalia before closing the door in her face.

"What's up, Fernando?" D-Boy was annoyed.

"What's going on with the girl? I thought you said she would stay here so you can keep an eye on her."

"There's a change in plans. Shorty is going back to her homeland of Morrocco. Over there, she poses no threat to your organization." D-Boy moved toward the door. "If you'll excuse me, she has a plane to catch."

Fernando stood in front of the door, stopping D-Boy from exiting the office. "Wait a minute. Who's to say that she can't give my information to someone like she did before? I need some assurance."

"Listen, there are some people involved who you don't want to rattle. It will only dismantle what you got going on. Shorty is no threat. I put my life on it." D-Boy gave him the look of a man who was serious.

Fernando moved from the door. "You're right. If she does violate, then your life is on the line, and I trust that you are not trying to go out over no bitch."

D-Boy didn't like his exchange with Fernando, but he had to play the game. "Facts. Now, like I said, excuse me. I'm escorting her to the airport. I'll see you when I return."

D-Boy brushed past Fernando to find Dalia still standing outside the office door.

"Is everything all right?" she asked, worried.

"Why wouldn't it be?" He moved toward the door. "Let's go before you miss your flight."

"I can't miss my flight because it's a private jet. They cannot leave until I show up."

"Excuse me. I forgot I was in the presence of a princess," he said playfully.

They walked to the black Mercedes being driven by Agent J, who always looked sinister. That was because his mind was always on his true mission: The Great Prophecy. He fantasized about getting the order to kill—all of them. His dick got hard just thinking about it. Sometimes, he had to go out and randomly kill to feed the growing urge. It was safe to say that Agent J was a certified sociopathic serial killer with a penchant for S&M.

The ride to the airport was quiet. They held hands while thinking about their future together. Being in a long-distance relationship where they were on different continents would be hard. However, if their love were true, it would transcend time and space.

When they arrived at the airport, D-Boy escorted her down the runway to the jet. Her mother, Queen Fatima, looked out of the plane and then hurried down the short steps to greet Dalia. She was flanked by her royal guards. She hugged Dalia, but she didn't hug her mother back. Her arms were just limp.

"Oh my God! Don't you ever do this again! I was worried sick about you. Did you know you were staying with drug dealers? We have to get you to a doctor to have you checked out. Who knows what bacteria and germs you've been exposed to."

"Mother, I'm fine."

The queen glanced over at D-Boy while rolling her eyes. "Who is this vagabond?"

"Mother! He is no vagabond. He saved my life."

"Apologies." She stuck out her hand for him to take it. "I am Queen Fatima Shahrah of Marrakesh. It is a pleasure to meet you."

D-Boy kissed the back of her hand and nodded his head in respect of royalty, something he had learned while in Dubai. "I am Darius Jensen. The pleasure is all mine, Your Highness."

"You are welcomed to accompany us back to the Royal Palace. I owe you my gratitude for rescuing my precious Dalia," Queen Fatima offered.

"I wish I could, but I have some pressing matters that I must address before I can take you up on your offer. May I take a raincheck?"

Queen Fatima was impressed by D-Boy's conduct. "You make sure that when you're free, you come to Marrakesh. You will have the time of your life. I'll guarantee it." She winked as if she was trying to hit on D-Boy.

"OK, Mother, you're pouring it on a little too thick, don't you think?" Dalia showed a tinge of jealousy.

"I'm just being hospitable to the man who saved my daughter's life." She smiled at D-Boy. "I'm going to let you two say your goodbyes. I hope to see you soon, Darius."

"Likewise, Your Highness."

She walked back up the short flight of steps and entered the jet with her royal guards in tow.

"She's a handful." Dalia rolled her eyes. "But I'm glad she likes you. She's hard to impress."

He pulled her in close to him. "Like mother like daughter." He kissed her. "I don't like long goodbyes. I'll see you soon. Take care of yourself." He detached himself and walked away.

Dalia watched him walk to the car. "Hey, D-Boy!" she yelled.

He stopped and turned around. "What's up?"

She ran up to him with open arms and hugged him with all her might. Then she kissed him like he was the only man in the world who mattered. "I love you."

"I love you too. Now, get on that jet and take your ass home." He smiled. "I'll see you soon." He got in the backseat of the Mercedes, and they drove away.

Dalia watched until he was out of her vision. Then she got on the jet, buckled her seat belt, and they took off headed for Marrakesh. Dalia looked out the window, lost in her thoughts of the last three weeks she spent with D-Boy.

Her mother watched her, knowing exactly what she was thinking about. "Don't worry. You'll see Darius again."

"D-Boy, I call him D-Boy." She lay back in the reclining seat and rested for the duration of the trip.

CHAPTER 10

ATLANTA JACKSON-HARTSFIELD INTERNATIONAL AIRPORT

DIRTY REDD just landed in Atlanta, excited about meeting this new woman named Jennifer. They texted often, but he only spoke on the phone with her twice. He found that odd but not enough to dismiss her. He liked the fact that she wasn't smothering him like most women. When he wanted to converse he would reach out on his time. After all, he considered himself the prize because he was famous.

"I just landed," Dirty Redd texted Jennifer.

"I can't wait to see you later," she responded.

"Me too, so you can do that thing you was talking about." He smiled.

"I'm going to suck your brains out." He got an erection when he read that message.

"So we're on for tonight at 8:00 p.m. I'll see you soon."

Dirty Redd stopped texting to call D-Boy. "What's popping? I'm in the ATL, my boy."

"You're in the ATL? What the fuck are you doing in Atlanta?" D-Boy said, concerned, because today was the day of the showdown with King Cobra.

"I had to sneak in to see this shorty."

"You always falling for a shorty. Today is not a good day to be in Atlanta," D-Boy informed him.

"What you mean? I told you I was coming."

"You told me you were coming two weeks ago. I'm just saying I can't get with you today. Maybe tomorrow." D-Boy couldn't tell him everything for his own safety.

"I get it. You got some top-secret shit going on. I will definitely get with you before I leave," Dirty Redd assured him before hanging up.

When Dirty Redd stepped out of the airport, he didn't notice the black Mercedes parked by the exit. Sarah was watching him. "Just as fine as the first day I met you."

When he got into his Uber, it drove him to his Airbnb. He got his things out of the trunk and entered the luxury apartment building. Sarah watched him the entire time, lusting after him. She couldn't help but get wet thinking about making love to him again. She sat in the seat, fantasizing about all the sex they used to have. At first, she was hypersexual for the mission. Then she started to like it so much she couldn't stop. That's when she fell in love with him.

"I wonder how he's going to act when he finds out his new friend 'Jennifer' is really me?" she said quietly before heading back to the safe house.

· · ·

DIAZ BROTHERS' MANSION

The three ex-Lost Souls soldiers were loading bullets into clips, preparing for the final showdown with King Cobra. It would be a slaughter because King Cobra had no idea he was about to be ambushed. Fernando wanted him to know that he and Diego took him out for their beloved uncle, Captain Diaz.

"I want to look him in his eyes before I blow his brains out," Diego said.

"We're both blowing his brains out. This has been a long time coming," Fernando replied.

They had so much firepower they could take on a platoon. They made sure they were well equipped for the job. They didn't want to get caught slipping like King Cobra, so they refused to count a victory before it happened. D-Boy was overseeing the whole operation from the invisible hand of John, the expert strategist. Without John's expertise, they would be going into this blind.

"Let's go over the plan one more time." D-Boy got everyone's attention. "You three are going to meet with him in the park. He's thinking you're still Lost Souls, so his guard will be down. That's when we will ambush him from all angles, and Fernando and Diego will handle their business."

They all nodded in agreement.

D-Boy looked at his watch. "Let's go. We have 30 minutes before showtime."

They all headed for the SUVs parked in the driveway.

KING COBRA'S HOUSE IN BUCKHEAD

Rodolfo was going over the plan with his handful of soldiers. There were 10 in all; he could call in reinforcements from other states. The Lost Souls cartel had 50,000 soldiers spread throughout the United States. At any given time, an army of Lost Souls could converge on you, and there was nothing you could do.

They thought they were just meeting with the three Lost Souls to be put on to a few of the Diaz brothers' spots. King Cobra wanted to be hands-on with taking over their operation. He usually sent soldiers to take care of business.

"I personally want to be there to seize their whole operation. It's satisfying for me to crush my opponents," King Cobra shouted to boost his men's morale.

"Let's head out. We're meeting our soldiers at this park, then headed to the first spot to put them on notice that the Lost Souls are here to take over this territory," Rodolfo stated.

They all hopped into the SUVs headed for Mount Morris Park, not knowing that this would be a showdown. Rodolfo was smart enough to have half of their soldiers stand back, so it appeared that the five men they pulled up with were all that came. This would catch the Diaz brothers off guard because they may be the ones getting a surprise.

As they pulled up, King Cobra saw the three Lost Souls standing in the parking lot. Rodolfo noticed a nervous tic on one of them as they got closer. He immediately started looking around, sensing something was fishy. He inched his way forward, and that's when he saw two men hiding in the bushes in his rearview mirror.

Rodolfo pulled out his 9 mm and cocked it back, ready to shoot. King Cobra noticed Rodolfo and became more alert. The two men in the bushes held fast to their positions, waiting for King Cobra to get out.

"Team 2, move in behind us. I think it's an ambush," Rodolfo said to the team 2 leader.

"An ambush?" King Cobra responded. "Why the fuck are we here?"

"We may be boxed in, but I'm killing these three traitors before we turn around." Rodolfo turned the car as if he was making a three-point turn and rolled the window down. The three men cracked a smile when they saw Rodolfo's familiar face.

When Rodolfo moved to get out of the car, he looked toward the bushes and saw the men coming out of hiding and moving forward. He just wanted to make sure that he was right before his next move.

Rodolfo took out his weapon and squeezed the trigger in the direction of the three men. "Fucking traitors!" he yelled out while multiple bullets sprayed them. He modified his gun to shoot like an Uzi, so all 30 bullets in his extended clip hit them fast. They all were cut down with one pull of the trigger.

He got back into the car and started making a U-turn. That's when the three men in the bushes, plus another three, came from the other side and advanced on the vehicle. They began spraying up the two SUVs, but to no avail because they were both fully armored. Before Rodolfo could complete turning around, Team 2 arrived and shot at the six men who were shooting at Rodolfo's vehicle. Rodolfo quickly turned the car around while the other vehicles just backed out. All three of the Lost Soul vehicles made it out of the ambush.

The Diaz brothers were in an SUV with D-Boy and Carlos on the corner, waiting for the signal to pull up and finish the job. They put two and two together when they saw King Cobra's cars racing away along with the gunshots.

"They got away," a soldier for the Diaz brothers reported.

"Fuck you mean they got away? How?" Fernando shouted.

"Somehow, they were prepared, so they were ready when we advanced on them."

"What about the three former Lost Souls?" Fernando asked.

"They all got hit, but they're still alive."

"Kill them. We don't need them anymore." Fernando ended communication.

"What happened?" Diego asked, hearing some of the conversation.

"He said they were on point and were ready for an ambush, but they got away."

"Fuck!" Diego yelled. "We may not get another chance to get him now because he's on point."

"Not necessarily," D-Boy chimed in. "I have my people trailing them as we speak." John was listening

John had already detached a drone to follow them to their hideout in Buckhead. It would only be a matter of hitting them there.

"I suggest we hit them now," John told D-Boy through the earpiece. "If we wait, it will give them a chance to be ready. If we attack now, they'll be caught off guard because they think no one knows where they are, giving us the advantage."

"I suggest we hit them now once we get their exact location because they won't get a chance to prepare because they think no one knows where they are. It gives us the upper hand." D-Boy relayed the same message to the Diaz brothers as if he were saying it himself.

"That's a fucking great idea, D-Boy," Fernando replied with enthusiasm.

The Diaz brothers did not know about John being in D-Boy's ear because his earpiece was the size of a tic-tac, making it impossible to see. It allowed John to be the unseen hand, something he learned to do from his years in Mossad.

Operations are better if they do not know you are there. The less people know, the better. It's the unseen "hand effect." D-Boy reflected on that lesson and now understood why it worked.

He was able to look at his phone. It showed him in real time where King Cobra was going. He gave Carlos the direction to drive. Twenty minutes later, King Cobra and his soldiers pulled up to the spacious mini-mansion. However, before they were about to press the code to open the door to the house, three black SUVs pulled up, and 12 men jumped out and began shooting at them.

King Cobra's men were being dropped before they could reach for their weapons. King Cobra caught two slugs in his rear shoulder, and Rodolfo was hit in his torso, but not before he could open the door, pull King Cobra in, and close the door. He saw that King Cobra was injured. Then he looked down and saw he was hit.

Blood gushed out. He needed something to stop the bleeding.

The Diaz brothers' soldiers made their way to the front door, giving head shots to any living Lost Soul still alive. When they reached the door, they shot it up. Then Fernando and Diego got out and walked up to the door.

"We have you surrounded, you fucking piece of shit," Fernando yelled. "You might as well come out and take your defeat like a man—that's *if* you are one."

"This is for our beloved Uncle Captain Diaz!" Diego added. "You killed a *real* soldier who was loyal to you. He would've died to protect you, and you killed him!"

"We can work this out!" King Cobra responded. "I will work for you if you let me live."

Rodolfo couldn't believe what he heard King Cobra say.

Here, I'm ready to die for you and with you, and you're a coward, Rodolfo thought.

He pointed his gun at King Cobra and snatched him to his feet. "Get the fuck up, coward!" He opened the front door. "Don't shoot! I'm coming out with this fucking snake under the condition that you let me live. I loved your uncle. Captain Diaz was like a father to all of us under this piece of shit." Rodolfo kicked him, and he winced as Rodolfo shoved him through the front door and came behind him with his hands up in the air.

Fernando grabbed him. "This is the day I've been waiting for. To avenge my uncle's death." He popped King Cobra in his head at close range, leaving brain matter splattered on the porch.

Diego shot him on the other side of his head, leaving

him looking like a smashed watermelon. "That was for my uncle, Captain Diaz. Now, he can rest in peace."

They looked at Rodolfo, his hands still in the air. "I never liked that piece of shit after he killed your uncle." Rodolfo spat on King Cobra's dead body.

"My uncle spoke highly of you on a few occasions," Fernando recalled. "And you were a friend to me and my brother."

"Let him live," Diego chimed in. "Besides, we can use a security detail with the knowledge of how a cartel works."

"You're right, Diego. I offered D-Boy the position, but I think Rodolfo is the man for the job since he ran the Lost Soul Cartel." Fernando stuck out his hand to Rodolfo to shake it, and he obliged.

"I promise to protect and die for the Diaz Brothers Cartel," Rodolfo declared.

"Then it's settled. Rodolfo is the new head of security for our cartel." Fernando made it official.

"Let's get the fuck out of here," D-Boy said, hearing sirens in the area.

They all hopped back into the vehicles with one extra person . . . Rodolfo, former lieutenant of the Lost Souls Cartel. He was now the head of security of the Diaz Brothers Cartel.

DIRTY REDD'S AIRBNB IN BUCKHEAD

Dirty Redd looked at the view of downtown Atlanta from the penthouse balcony. He was anxious to meet his new concubine. The anticipation had been building up for weeks. He liked to meet new women under these circumstances. He was so used to getting any woman he chose from concerts and enjoyed the mystery of this meeting with Jennifer.

He was a sucker for love who wore his heart on his sleeve. He accepted his shortcomings as a part of who he was as a man. He fell in love quickly and fell out of love just as fast. It was a gift and a curse for him. The gift was not being afraid to love, and the curse was loving so easily. It wasn't the worst character trait as long as he knew what it was so he could deal with it.

His phone rang. It was Jennifer. "Hey, baby, I'm downstairs in the lobby."

"OK, I'm going to come down to get you." He put on his Billigoat leather and walked to the elevator. "Finally, I get to meet you in person."

"I know, right? It's been my dream come true," she responded.

His phone service went out when he got on the elevator. He pressed the button to get to the lobby. When the door opened, several people stood around talking and having drinks at the bar. He looked around, trying to find a woman who resembled Jennifer.

"Where is she at?" He swiveled his head and stared at every girl.

He didn't see Sarah sneak up behind him until she tapped him on his shoulder. "I'm behind you."

Dirty Redd turned around slowly. When he saw the face of the woman standing there, he gasped. It was like he saw a ghost. "Sarah, what the fuck are you doing here?" He was bewildered. "How did you know I was here?" He still didn't get it that Sarah was Jennifer.

"Let me explain." She paused, and he stared at her, confused. "I'm Jennifer. I did it to see you without causing confusion."

"Without causing confusion?" He shook his head. "You disappeared on me right after you dropped the bomb on me that you were pregnant with my baby."

"Can we go somewhere private? It's not safe for us to be seen like this. The Agency has eyes everywhere."

He turned around, and she followed him onto the elevator. He pressed the button, and it stopped on the penthouse floor. When they entered the apartment, Sarah pressed Dirty Redd against the wall and started unzipping his pants while kissing him. At first, he resisted her advance, but he gave in when she grabbed his penis.

"I missed you," she said while getting down on her knees and stuffed his manhood into her mouth.

"Ohh, I missed that mouth," he responded.

"I dreamed every night of doing this to you." She spoke with his whole dick in her mouth.

The vibration of her phone interrupted her, but she answered without stopping.

"Where are you?" Heron asked suspiciously.

"Remember I told you I was hanging out with my girlfriend, Jennifer?" She sucked him. "You're the one that suggested it, remember?" she sucked him some more while waiting for a response.

"You're right, babe. I did tell you to go out because you were getting cranky around the house." He paused because he heard something. "What's that noise?"

"What noise?" she stopped sucking.

"It was some static or something, but it went away. Be safe. You are with child, but enjoy your outing with your friend." Heron waited for her to respond, but she was busy sucking again, "Babe?"

"Yes, honey. You were breaking up. I'll be safe and enjoy myself. Thank you for suggesting it. It's definitely what I needed. I'll see you later. Love ya." She slurped again.

"Love you too, babe."

She ended the call after she waited for him to tell her he loved her too. She was a master of reading Heron's emotions. He was so far up her ass he didn't know whether he was coming or going. He was the easiest mark for Sarah because he was so arrogant he couldn't conceive the thought that he was being played.

She looked at Dirty Redd's stiff, hard penis. "Now, where was I?" she returned to her regularly scheduled program.

CHAPTER 11
YC'S MANSION IN ALPHARETTA, GEORGIA

YC COULDN'T GET his last conversation with D-Boy out of his mind. He was one of those people who wouldn't stop until he got to the bottom of a situation. His intuition was screaming that D-Boy was really his second cousin, that they were blood. To YC, nothing had a stronger bond than blood. Plus, he didn't know most of his family on his mother's side, which made him want to know any family members he did have.

He was determined to get to the truth. He was searching the internet for proof that D-Boy was Darius Jensen. He saw the way D-Boy acted when he first approached him about it. He was taken aback by the question. He kept searching the internet, hoping to find a connection between the two.

He didn't know that John had the entire internet swept clean of his and D-Boy's pictures on social media. What John couldn't delete was the post that someone shared. He couldn't delete everything, just the posts he could find.

This was why YC found a post from a club that Jay-Roc was DJing at. He saw the pic and blew it up to enlarge it, and sure enough, there was D-Boy standing beside Jay-Roc.

"Who is Jay-Roc to D-Boy?" YC asked himself. "There has to be a connection between the two."

YC decided to switch subjects and look into Jay-Roc. Jay-Roc was easier to investigate because he was a public figure. He was known as one of the most successful CEOs in hip-hop history. Anyone who followed the inner workings of the music industry knew Jay-Roc Jensen. What caught his attention was that he was the CEO behind the Billigoats, his arch nemesis.

"Fuck the Billigoats," YC said as he learned the information that Jay-Roc had ties with them. "Cuz or no cuz, I don't rock with them. I don't care if we are blood." He saw pictures of Jay-Roc with the Billigoats.

All it took was for YC to look into Jay-Roc, and he found the evidence he was looking for in no time. It was an article with Jay-Roc speaking about the death of his little brother, D-Boy, and how that was his only brother. Then there was a picture of the two standing beside each other.

It was unmistakable that the D-Boy at the Diaz mansion was the same Darius "D-Boy" Jensen who was murdered 11 years ago. He blew up the picture and stared at it to make sure he was accurate. He was going to approach D-Boy about his discovery. How he reacts will determine YC's next move.

"I wonder why he's acting like he isn't my cousin and lying about who he is." That was the million-dollar question on YC's mind. "I'm going to get to the bottom of this shit like I always do." He jumped into his car and headed for the Diaz mansion to confront D-Boy in person.

As YC was driving on Interstate 85 North toward the Diaz mansion, he got a call from Fernando. "What up, my brother?"

"I'm calling an emergency meeting. I need you here ASAP." Fernando spoke with concern.

"What's going on?" YC asked, noticing his tone.

"Nothing I want to discuss over the phone. Just get here as fast as you can." Fernando hung up.

I wonder what it is now, YC thought.

When YC pulled up and walked through the front door, the first person he encountered was D-Boy. YC smiled when he saw him because he knew the truth: D-Boy was Darius Jensen, his second cousin. There was nothing that D-Boy could tell him to make him believe otherwise. Now, YC just wanted to know the whole truth.

D-Boy noticed the smile on YC's face. It gave him vibes that he knew something. He recalled his last conversation with YC when he was investigating D-Boy's existence. YC had the demeanor of a man who had cracked the code, and the smile on his face confirmed his victory.

"What's popping, YC?" D-Boy broke the ice by speaking first.

"I don't know. You tell me, Darius."

"Darius?" D-Boy heard John chime into his ear.

"He knows, and contrary to what I taught you, it's strategic for us to tell YC the truth. We can make him our ally. He could be a formidable force."

D-Boy listened to John and nodded in agreement. YC thought he was nodding at him, so his smile broadened.

D-Boy started walking toward his room. "Come to my room so we can talk in private."

YC followed him and waited for the door to close. "So, you admit you are my second cousin, Darius Jensen?"

D-Boy looked around him. "You have to be very careful with that information. Yes, I'm your second cousin, Darius Jensen, but no one can know that. The reason I'm telling you is to save your life."

"You're saving my life? From whom?" YC got serious.

"The CIA, for one. They are the ones who are shipping the Nitro into the United States. They are the reason that I had to fake my death, and you are working for the same people that I'm fighting against. They are using you as a pawn, and when they finish with you, they will either murder you or send you away to prison for life." D-Boy looked directly into YC's eyes as his words settled.

YC knew D-Boy was telling him the truth. Now, his mind was racing. "So, what the fuck do I do? Fake my death too? I'm knee-deep in this shit with the Diaz brothers. Do they know they're working with the CIA?"

"No, and it's better that way because they cover their tracks with secrecy. If the Diaz brothers knew, they'd already be dead." D-Boy saw the confusion on YC's face. "Just play the role, business as usual. I'll let you know when it's time to make a move. I will make sure the Agency won't hurt any more of my family members again. Guard this secret with your life because you *will* die if you say anything about what I just told you."

YC knew he wasn't playing any games. "I got you, Cuz." He gave D-Boy a firm handshake. "It's an honor to be related to you, Big Cuz. From what I learned, you were the man up in New York, the biggest in the city."

"One day, I'll tell you all about it, but for now, let's stick to the plan, which is silence and patience until I give you the signal," D-Boy instructed.

"I got you, Big Cuz." YC exited the room and headed toward the office to meet up with Fernando. He was still intrigued about this "Emergency Meeting."

When he entered the office, Diego, Carlos, and Fernando greeted him. Then D-Boy strolled in, and that's when the meeting started. D-Boy already knew what the meeting was about because he was tasked with delivering messages from Heron to the Diaz brothers. That's how Heron distanced himself from all activities . . . by using a third party.

"I have good news and bad news. Let me give you the bad news first." Fernando paused. "We cannot produce Nitro fast enough in the territory where we grow it. We need more land to grow more Nitro, so me and Diego are going to Colombia to acquire all the fields from the Lost Souls Cartel. We need to acquire more fields because D-Boy has informed me that our shipping partners see the demand and have made provisions to ship twice the amount into the country."

YC glanced at D-Boy, keeping their previous conversation in mind. Now that he knew that the CIA was involved, it all made perfect sense how tons were being shipped into the country. He also knew that he was in over his head, and silence was his only protection.

"While we're in Colombia taking care of the land grab,

I'm leaving YC in charge of operations until we get back," Fernando announced.

"I appreciate the offer, but I'm dropping a new album that needs promotion. I don't know if I can be 100 percent available," YC replied.

Fernando thought for a second. "OK, Carlos will be your number two when you have to promote your new album."

"That'll work," Carlos chimed in.

"So, it's a done deal. YC and Carlos will run the business while me and Fernando are back home in Colombia," Diego said.

"Our flight for Colombia leaves tomorrow morning. Good luck." Fernando shook YC's hand as confirmation.

"I don't believe in luck. I got this," YC responded.

When the men dispersed from the office, D-Boy went to his room to speak privately with John. John heard the whole conversation and was already putting together a plan. They didn't have much time. Grandpa Joe's life was in danger every day he was held captive by Heron.

"You heard that?" D-Boy asked John.

"Loud and clear. A few things come to mind. The first thing was how Heron was putting the Diaz brothers in a position to be the number one cartel in the world. Taking out King Cobra made the Diaz brothers the only cartel that could supply Agent Heron. Any dealing with Heron is dangerous because he's unpredictable. Once he finds out the formula for Nitro, he will cut the Diaz brothers out of the equation."

D-Boy never interrupted John. "I have an idea. Why don't we take a sample of Nitro to find out the chemical compound that is the secret ingredient? I know your super-computer can break it down."

"You know what, D-Boy? That's ingenious. You're right. My computer can break it down and separate the ingredients. We can use it as leverage to save Grandpa Joe, and once he's safe, we can take out Heron once and for all."

"*That's* what the fuck I'm talking about. Let's get to it to take this motherfucker out." D-Boy was excited about the prospect of killing Heron once and for all.

"It'll take my system at least a week to break everything down. In the meantime, stay cool. We don't want to blow up our plans."

"I'll meet you at that same gas station we met at a week ago to give you a sample of Nitro."

It's been a whole month since Dalia left for Marrakesh. I miss her, D-Boy thought.

As if on cue, D-Boy's phone rang. It was Dalia. "Let me take this call. I'll meet you in an hour." D-Boy hung up with John and connected the call with Dalia. "Hey, baby, how's Marrakesh?"

"I miss you so much, D-Boy." She bit her lip. "All I think about is you. I can't eat, and I can't sleep. I need you."

"Don't worry. We'll be together soon. It's great to hear from you."

"Likewise. I was trying not to bother you because I know you're busy trying to fix that situation."

"It'll all be over soon, and then we'll be together. I've been thinking about moving to Marrakesh and getting dual citizenship."

Dalia smiled. "I would love that. Hurry up and fix it so you can come home to me."

"I got you. Let me call you back later today. I have to do something important."

"OK, I love you, D-Boy." She waited for him to reciprocate, but he paused. "You're not going to say you love me back?"

"Of course. I was just thinking how much I love you before I responded. I love you more. I'll talk to you later." D-Boy hung up.

He had to get his hands on some Nitro without raising suspicion. He only needed an ounce, but an ounce was $2,500. The last thing he needed was someone trying to investigate him like YC did. He had more to lose than anyone else because his grandfather's life was on the line.

He needed the code to the storage room in the garage where they stored enough to distribute from the mansion. He was about to ask Fernando but knew it would raise suspicions. Then it dawned on him to ask John.

"John, you there?"

John was analyzing the layout of the safe house, trying to figure out a way to disable the alarm system. "Yes, sir, what's going on?"

"I need you to crack the code on the storage room in the four-car garage so I can get you that ounce of Nitro."

John pulled up the schematics of the Diaz brothers' mansion in 3-D and quickly navigated to the storage. In a matter of seconds, he cracked the code of the Nitro storage room.

"That was fast," D-Boy said, walking in and seeing

racks of bricks wrapped tight, weighing a kilo apiece. There had to be at least 500 kilos in the storage.

The only problem was that none were opened, and D-Boy could not weigh an ounce. He had to think fast.

"D-Boy, you got company coming your way," John informed him by looking at the 3-D view of the mansion. "It looks like Diego. He's 200 feet from the garage. Get out of there!"

D-Boy grabbed one of the bricks, stuffed it in his pants, and put his shirt over the lump protruding from his waist. He knew he would run into Diego on his way out of the garage, so he grabbed a set of keys and started the Rolls-Royce Wraith with the key. As Diego entered the garage, D-Boy opened the door and got in.

"Damn, I was about to take the Wraith out today," Diego said right before D-Boy sat in the driver's seat.

"You can take it. I'll take the Lambo truck. I haven't driven that one yet." D-Boy moved to give Diego the keys and his shirt lifted up slightly, revealing the brick of Nitro.

Diego saw the brick right before D-Boy lowered his shirt over the top of the brick in his pants. It was obvious that D-Boy was in the area where the bricks were stored, and now he had one in his pants. D-Boy knew he was caught by how Diego looked at him with suspicion.

I should've just sat in the car and driven off. I can't turn back now. I'll pretend like he didn't see it. I have to save Grandpa Joe, D-Boy thought before quickly grabbing the Lambo truck's keys.

Diego followed him with his eyes as he got into the vehicle. He didn't sit in the driver's seat of the Wraith. D-Boy saw Diego watching him as he opened the garage, drove to the front gate, and waited for it to open. Diego shook his head as he thought about what he had just seen.

This motherfucker is stealing from us.

Diego took out his phone and called Fernando. "I just saw D-Boy in the garage by the storage room. He was about to take the Wraith out until I said I would take it. Then I saw a brick of Nitro sticking out of his pants."

Fernando thought before speaking. "What did he say to you? Was he acting suspicious?"

"He didn't say anything. He was in a rush, so, yes, he was acting suspicious because he had a brick of Nitro in his fucking pants!" Diego responded angrily.

"Let's look at the footage before we jump to conclusions. Rodolfo just put hidden cameras by the storage room and all around the house. If he's on camera going into the storage room, then we know he's stealing from us." Fernando was pleased with Rodolfo's performance as their head of security.

"That's fair. It could've been something else sticking out of his pants that looked like a brick of Nitro," Diego said, agreeing with Fernando. "Tell Rodolfo to check the footage at . . ." He looked at his Rolex, "like 15 minutes ago, so like 1:30."

"Got you." Fernando hung up and called Rodolfo. "Check the camera footage from the storage in the garage for around 1:30 today, about 20 minutes ago."

"I'm on it," Rodolfo replied.

"I THINK Diego saw the brick in my pants when I turned

around to give him the keys to the Wraith. He stared at me like I was crazy," D-Boy informed John.

John was seven steps ahead of him. He saw the exchange between D-Boy and Diego, and he was already hacking into the new security system that Rodolfo installed. He looped five seconds of the footage and replaced the footage of D-Boy going in and out of the storage.

"I got this. Just meet me at the QT gas station with the brick. It will take me some time to break it down to discover the formula."

D-Boy met John at the gas station with the drug. He knew the close call with Diego could've botched the whole mission and killed Grandpa Joe. He thought every day about Grandpa Joe's state of mind being locked up in that room all day. His life was in danger every moment he was held hostage by Heron.

D-Boy entered the same bathroom and saw a man at the stall. "John, this shit is getting too close for comfort. Grandpa Joe's life is on the line."

"Excuse me, but I'm not John. Sorry to hear about your Grandpa Joe, though." The man finished urinating and washed his hands, then exited the bathroom.

I'm losing it. I could've sworn that it was John in one of his disguises, D-Boy thought as another strange-looking man entered the bathroom.

"Good day to do some fly fishing," the man said to D-Boy for no reason.

"John?" D-Boy had to make sure this guy was John after what had just happened. He could never tell.

"Excuse me," the man said. "My name is Samuel. You have me mistaken for someone else."

"Pardon me, I thought you were my friend John." D-Boy strolled toward the exit.

"D-Boy," the man said.

"Fuck. I never know which disguise you're going to wear. You're getting too good at this."

"That's the objective. If I can fool you, then I can fool anyone," John responded.

This disguise made him appear like a Mexican migrant worker. It was masterfully crafted to make John look like he had been landscaping all day. Even if someone paid you, you could never figure out one of John's many disguises.

D-Boy handed John the brick of Nitro. "This shit almost got me caught, which could've got Grandpa Joe killed. What's the plan to get him free? I know you have something up your sleeve."

"They have an advanced security system that my super-computer can't hack. We will have to walk in announced so that the landmines are off. The safe house is virtually impenetrable." John saw D-Boy's facial expression show disappointment and doubt.

"So, this plan to discover the formula and give it to Heron is all we got." D-Boy was trying to find the silver lining in the dark cloud.

"It looks like that's the best plan so far. And just to think, my student came up with it is amazing. You've come a long way from hustling on the block." John patted D-Boy on the back.

"Fuck all that. I'm not satisfied until Grandpa Joe is safe and sound and Heron is rotting in his grave."

"We can't get close enough to Heron to kill him. Until

we free Grandpa Joe, he holds all the cards. We can't risk taking Heron out before rescuing Grandpa Joe first."

"So, cracking the code on the secret ingredients of Nitro is our only hope at saving Grandpa Joe?" D-Boy asked, knowing the answer to his question.

"That's how it looks for now unless something new comes up."

D-Boy looked at his watch. "Let me get back to the mansion and defuse the situation about the brick of Nitro." D-Boy gave John a handshake. "See you soon." He exited the bathroom.

John didn't want to say it, but Agent J was the real problem. At any given time, Agent J could be given the order, and everyone in the safe house would be murdered. John knew a lot about the Great Prophecy and the dangers it presented to the world. If they are successful, then every man, woman, and child will be slaves to the Zionists.

Even though John was Jewish, he didn't consider himself a Zionist. He knew the truth about his people, and he regarded Zionism as a threat to everyone, Jews included. The appearance of Agent J here in America working with Heron meant only one thing: the Great Prophecy had begun; it was only a matter of time before it was in full effect mode.

The Zionists must be stopped by any means necessary, John thought as he exited the bathroom.

CHAPTER 12
LENOX MALL

Dirty Redd pulled up to the Lenox Mall valet in a baby blue Corvette that he had rented for the week he was in Atlanta. He was a famous rapper, so heads turned when they noticed one-third of the Billigoats getting out of the vehicle. People took out their phones and went live, showing Dirty Redd walking into the mall. He signed a few autographs as he walked through the entrance.

Police saw the commotion and closely watched the crowd gathering around the famous rapper. Lenox Mall was known for having celebrities strolling through it. They were one of the only malls in the South with every major clothing brand in its halls. People from all around the South visited Lenox to get the latest Gucci, Prada, Fendi, and Louis Vuitton.

One of the spectators was a member of YC's Blood set. He knew that YC had some issues with the members of the Billigoats. He watched Dirty Redd signing autographs and greeting fans, so he took out his phone and FaceTimed YC.

"What up, fool?" YC greeted his comrade with their gang vernacular.

"Hey, I'm at Lenox Mall, and this dude, Dirty Redd from the Billigoats, is here getting love from the people." He showed Dirty Redd signing autographs on the screen.

"Oh, this nigga thinks he's safe in my hood? I'm about to pull up on his bitch ass." YC hung up the phone and jumped in his new Lamborghini Revuelto.

His new Lambo was so fast that it got him there in 10 minutes. It was usually a 25-minute drive from his mansion in Alpharetta. When he pulled up to the valet, a group of onlookers started filming him live.

"That's YC! YC, I love you!" a young female fan yelled.

"I love you too," he said as he rushed through the entrance to get to Dirty Redd.

YC walked quickly toward the area where Dirty Redd was mingling with fans. He saw him surrounded by fans taking pictures and signing autographs. Some fans saw YC approaching the crowd. Everyone knew about the beef between him and the Billigoats. Right before YC reached the circle of people, Dirty Redd saw him, and his eyes widened at the sight of him running down on him.

Dirty Redd knew he was at a disadvantage being in YC's hometown of Atlanta. He also knew cameras were on them, so whatever he did would be televised. He couldn't go out like no sucker, but he also wasn't stupid. Dirty Redd braced himself for the worst, knowing that the beef between them was real and just getting started.

"What up, YC?" Dirty Redd said, breaking the ice.

"What's up? You know what the fuck is up. You know

it's not safe for you in my hood. You lucky all these police are here because it wouldn't be nice for you."

"Fuck the police, nigga. Me and you can get it popping one-on-one." Dirty Redd threw his hands up.

He didn't see the guy coming up behind him, but he punched Dirty Redd on the back of his head, causing him to fall forward into YC. YC then punched him twice in the face, thrusting him backward. It was two-on-one, and they were giving Dirty Redd the business. Both men were beating him all about the head and body until the police finally broke it up. They were slow in interfering because a few police officers were routing for YC since he was at a home-field advantage.

"You got that one. You had to jump me, though, because you know one-on-one I would beat your ass." Dirty Redd spit some blood from his mouth as he spoke.

"Look at you, all fucked up. That's what you get for thinking shit sweet in the A. Take your bitch ass back to New York." YC was half laughing at Dirty Redd.

"It's on! You know you can't come to New York."

"I got a show up there this weekend! You ain't going to do nothing," YC replied.

"We'll see." Dirty Redd was escorted out of the mall by Atlanta Police.

Several spectators caught the whole altercation on camera. It didn't look good for Dirty Redd to get jumped. It only opened up a can of worms that would become messy. Both teams were strong in the music industry, with resources and soldiers in both places.

The fight between YC and Dirty Redd went viral on social media. It didn't take two hours before news of the skirmish spread to D-Boy and John. They had interests on both sides of the conflict: Dirty Redd was a part of the American D-Boy Records family, and YC was family through blood. But D-Boy wasn't taking sides. Dirty Redd was part of his business, and although he had just met YC, he liked his style, besides the fact that he was his second cousin.

"You see this shit?" D-Boy asked John.

"Yeah, it's pretty bad. You have to defuse this before it worsens," he advised.

D-Boy called Dirty Redd. "Yo, I saw what happened at Lenox Mall. You all right?"

"It's on! He better not ever come to New York. I promise you he won't leave in one piece." Dirty Redd was fuming.

"I understand, but you have to use your head on this one. You can throw it all away over a misunderstanding."

"Fuck a misunderstanding! They *jumped* me. You are talking like you on his side or something." Dirty Redd noticed D-Boy making excuses for YC.

"I just don't want to see two brothers kill each other over nothing." D-Boy would feel the same way.

"I'm at the penthouse about to get myself together. I'll call you later." Dirty Redd hung up.

Dirty Redd was back at his penthouse suite. Before he could take off his shoes, Sarah knocked on his door. "Baby, it's me." He opened the door, and she hugged him. "Are you all right?"

"I'm fine; nothing to a G." He went to the bathroom to run some hot water.

"Let me help you, baby." Sarah put a washcloth in the

water and wiped the blood from his face. "I saw the whole thing live on social media. It's going viral on every platform."

"He got that one, but it's just getting started."

Mouf called, and Dirty Redd picked up on the first ring. "Yo, I saw that shit. I already contacted my people in Atlanta. It's on and popping." Mouf was very upset about his partner in rhyme getting jumped.

"I's all good because sucker know he can't whoop me. That's why he had to jump me."

"What you wanna do? I can be on the next flight, and we can step to him like men and get that one-on-one. I know you can beat YC. He knows it too. That's why they had to jump you."

"Don't come down here. I'm leaving here tomorrow." Sarah suddenly got sad when he announced his departure, but she said nothing.

"OK, I'll see you tomorrow." Mouf hung up.

Sarah was nursing his wounds when she noticed her phone was ringing, but it was on silent. It was Heron, but she didn't want to talk to him. Attending to Dirty Redd was more important to her. Even though she knew not to play with Heron, her heart was saying fuck him. She wanted to stay with Dirty Redd for the night since he was leaving in the morning. Doing that could mean suicide for her, but she was willing to take the risk.

"I want to stay with you tonight." She kissed his forehead.

"I don't think that's a good idea. Wouldn't what's his name come looking for you?"

"His name is Heron, and yes, he will come looking for

me. I just have to come up with a good story." Sarah looked worried, and Dirty Redd noticed it.

"No, I'm not letting you risk your life. We will see each other again, I promise." He kissed her passionately.

"I love you, Dirty Redd." Sarah shed a tear and kissed him. "You're right. I can't stay the night. He'll send a squad to find me and kill us both." She closed her eyes and kissed him.

"You know there's only one way for us to be together, right?" He paused and looked at her. "You have to kill Heron. He is the problem for you and for my people, Jay-Roc and D-Boy." He stared at her to see her response.

"You're right. Someone has to do it, and I'm closest to him. He's in love with me, but I loathe the sight of him," she admitted.

"I mean, you are the only one close to him that he trusts. Think about it. You'll be doing everyone a favor."

Sarah thought about it. She knew he was right, but it wouldn't be easy. Heron was protected by the most powerful agency on the planet. She knew that they would come after her if she assassinated Heron. He was a high-ranking agent that the Agency valued because of his advanced intel skills.

"I have to think about that one because no one will be safe, not me, not you, or our baby." Sarah smiled. "I can feel him moving sometimes."

"How do you know it's a boy? Did you ask for the gender?" Dirty Redd asked.

"Not yet, I just feel it." She saw him wince in pain from a sudden movement. "Relax yourself. You just survived a major attack. You need to rest and heal. I wish I could stay, but he's already calling. Soon, he'll send out a search party." She kissed him. "I'll see you later tonight."

"You know I leave tomorrow at noon?"

She stopped at the door. "I hate that you have to go. Why can't you just move to Atlanta?"

"New York is my home; the South is too slow for me. I need the hustle and bustle of the Big Apple," Dirty Redd replied sincerely.

"I'll see you at 9:00 sharp. I love you, Dirty Redd." She didn't wait to hear his response before she left the suite.

Sarah got on the elevator and walked to the black Mercedes-Benz parked in the parking lot. She didn't see Agent J sitting in a work van that had Cohen Cleaning Service on the side. Mossad provided this for him, and it was equipped with the latest surveillance technology. It was very similar to what John had in the Warlord. But John upgraded the technology that Agent J had so John's was superior. Both Agent J's van and the Warlord were built for destruction. Agent J's had an arsenal capable of taking out a platoon.

Agent J didn't need to follow her. He knew where she was going. He had to narrow down the guest list here to figure out who she was seeing. He used the GPS he hid in the Benz trunk to follow her to the hotel but didn't know what room she was in. He didn't want to expose himself by getting out on foot because she would surely spot him.

The supercomputer in his vehicle was going through the list of guests and comparing it to any anomaly that occurred. It narrowed down the list to 10 names with pictures of their driver's licenses. The computer lit up on one of the names with a message that read Possible Hit.

The name was Alen Aldridge Jr. He was 34 years old, and his alias read Dirty Redd.

Agent J scratched his chin. "I know that name from the file on D-Boy." He paused before initiating a command to his supercomputer. "Pull up images of everything pertaining to D-Boy."

Images popped up for five seconds at a time, pics going back to D-Boy's first and only arrest when he was 12. The public dubbed him "The Baby Face Killer" because he was a suspect in a homicide. Then pictures of the Billigoats emerged.

"Stop," he commanded when he saw the picture of Dirty Redd. "That's my guy right there."

He sat thinking about what he knew of the operation that Sarah was on in Dubai. He didn't know the specifics but remembered she was on a catch-and-kiss mission. Her mission was top secret, but there was nothing really secret in the Agency. All he needed to do was show the picture to Heron, and he would know. Besides, Heron is the one who told Agent J to follow Sarah because he was suspicious of her actions lately.

Agent J liked to sow seeds of deception and separation within the Agency. It made it easier for him to carry out his mission when the Great Prophecy got underway. He was almost certain that Dirty Redd had something to do with Sarah.

Agent J sent the pic of Dirty Redd to Heron, and then he called him. "Does this guy have anything to do with Sarah?"

Heron took a deep breath and closed his eyes. "Yes.

Sarah was romantically involved with him on her mission in Dubai."

"She just left a hotel. An Alen Aldridge, aka Dirty Redd, was listed as one of the patrons staying here. I couldn't get close enough to confirm that she was seeing him, but I don't believe in coincidences either."

"Neither do I." Heron shook his head. "Thank you for the info." Then he hung up.

I knew something was up with her the way she's been so cold to me, he thought.

He sat in his chair, lit a cigar, then took a healthy pull and put it out. He was angry, not because she was seeing another man, but because the other man was a Black man. His face turned beet red as he thought about Sarah being with Dirty Redd off the mission grid. He developed feelings for Sarah quickly, but just as fast, he was ready to kill her. The psychopath in him was waking up. He was pondering ways to kill her slowly.

As he was contemplating torture techniques, she entered the front door. "Honey, I'm home," she shouted.

Heron came around the corner to greet her with a hug and a kiss, pretending not to know anything about her whereabouts. "Hey, honey, how was your day out?"

"It was not all it was cracked up to be. I didn't buy anything there." She glanced at Heron, noticing he was unusually happy. "What's going on? I haven't seen you smiling this much since I told you I was pregnant."

"I was just thinking about retiring and you and I moving to a remote island in the Pacific." Heron was testing her to see her reaction.

She didn't get excited. *I would rather commit suicide than be alone with you on a remote island*, she thought.

Heron saw her facial expression go blank. "Is there something wrong? You look like you smell something rank." He could read her mind.

Come on, get it together, she thought.

"I would love that. Me, you, and the baby on an island all by ourselves." She kissed and hugged him.

I know you're full of shit, Heron thought as he looked at his reflection in the mirror on the wall.

"I'm going to go lie down. I'm so tired; this baby is kicking my ass." Sarah walked past Heron to their room, where she lay down and closed her eyes.

How can I kill Heron without getting caught? she thought before setting her alarm for 8:00 p.m. *I can't wait to see Dirty Redd tonight.*

Her alarm went off, and she couldn't believe the time went that fast. She got up, took a quick shower, and put on sexy lingerie. Then she put on a sweatsuit over the lingerie to disguise it from Heron. She came up with a good enough excuse to get out. She told him that her phony friends begged her to hang out with them tonight. Every agent had phony friends to throw anyone from the trail if they snooped around. All agents needed regular people in their lives to appear normal to the general public. It was a tactic used to have some regular activity in the lives of agents out in the field for long periods.

Heron was in his office. "Hey, babe, the girls begged me to come out with them tonight. We're doing karaoke at Duggans in Midtown."

"Have fun," Heron smiled. "Make sure you're being safe out there."

"I will." She kissed him on the forehead, left the safe house, and headed for Dirty Redd's penthouse suite.

When she left, Heron called Agent J into his office. "She just left. Follow her, and when I give you the call, I want you to go to the room listed in Dirty Redd's name and kill them both."

"Are you sure you want me to kill Agent Sarah?" Agent J asked, confused.

"She's no good to me after she lied to me to be with a nigger." Heron lit a cigar. "Don't make her suffer. Make it quick." He let out a plume of smoke.

"I got you, but Dirty Redd will die slowly. I hate niggers too."

"Whatever, just don't let Sarah suffer." Heron fought back the tears until Agent J left the office. Then he browsed through pictures of Sarah on his phone. "We could've ruled the world together, and you threw it all away for a two-bit nigger." The tears flowed, but minutes later, Heron wiped them and shut off his feelings for her that fast. It was a technique he learned in the CIA boot camp.

Heron went to the minibar in the office, poured himself a shot of bourbon, and quickly tossed it down. "Farewell, Red Sparrow." That was the code name he gave Sarah when he first recruited her into the Agency.

He had pictures of several female prospects to recruit in Sarah's place. He stopped at a redhead who resembled Sarah, except she was curvier. Heron studied her profile; he liked what her bio said about her. She had a black belt in karate and scored 100 on the aptitude test.

"She is an agent created in CIA heaven." Heron called the number on her profile. "Hello, may I speak to Tammy?"

"This is Tammy. Who am I speaking with?"

"My name is George, and I have the opportunity of a lifetime for you. How would you like to be an agent with the Central Intelligence Agency?" The silence was deafening.

"Is this a joke?" Tammy was a no-nonsense woman.

"No, ma'am. You took a test with the New York State Troopers and aced it. That's how I got wind of you."

Tammy knew he was telling the truth about her aptitude test with the NYS Troopers. Her whole life, she has wanted to be in law enforcement. She liked the thought of having power over the average civilian. She was a bit of a narcissist who had to feed her ego. Perfect for the Agency.

"I don't know what to say."

"I'll take that as a yes." Heron smiled. "A plane ticket to Atlanta, Georgia, was just sent to your email along with basic instructions. If you should accept, a cash advance of $50K will be wired to your account as your first payment."

"Fifty thousand!" Tammy didn't have to think twice. "I'm all in."

"Great. I'll see you tomorrow." Heron ended the call.

They all fall for the $50K, not knowing it's a down payment for their soul, he thought as he poured another shot of the bourbon.

CHAPTER 13
DIRTY REDD'S PENTHOUSE

IT WAS ten minutes to 9:00. Dirty Redd anxiously awaited Sarah's return as promised. He couldn't wait to spend his last night in Atlanta with her. The dangerous nature of their relationship turned them both on.

At exactly 8:59, someone knocked on the door. Dirty Redd rushed to open it. Sarah was standing there, smiling, before she entered the suite. She wasted no time unfastening his belt and pants, then pulled them down. Then she got on her knees and performed fellatio as if her life depended on it.

"That shit feels so good," he moaned.

She didn't skip a beat when she heard his phone ringing. She tried to stop him from answering it. "Don't answer it." She bobbed her head faster. "Wait until you explode in my mouth."

The phone kept ringing.

THE DIAZ MANSION

D-Boy was in panic mode, listening to the phone ring. "Pick up the fucking phone!"

John was listening. "He doesn't even know his life is in danger."

John had 24-hour surveillance on the safe house and noticed more movement than usual. They didn't leave in more than one vehicle at a time, but he noticed Sarah being followed two days in a row to the same hotel. Agent J followed her yesterday in the Cohen Cleaning Service van he knew was provided by Mossad. John learned that whenever there's a glitch, there is a reason for it.

He took it upon himself to see if anyone was staying at that hotel that had some connection. When he looked at the guest list and saw Dirty Redd's government name, he knew who it was. It didn't take him long to surmise that Sarah was there to meet secretly with Dirty Redd. Then he thought about Agent J following her twice.

"Either Agent J is there to watch her back, or he's following her, and she doesn't know it." He contemplated a bit, then concluded that Sarah was meeting with Dirty Redd, and she didn't know she was being watched.

John immediately called D-Boy. "Call Dirty Redd ASAP!"

"What's going on?"

"Sarah went to his hotel two days in a row and was followed. She doesn't know that her secret is out, and Agent J is there, which could mean Dirty Redd's life is in danger."

D-Boy immediately called Dirty Redd. "Come on, pick

up. Out of all the times that you pick up on the first ring, you pick today not to answer."

D-Boy tried calling again but to no avail. He was about to try again, but his phone started ringing. "What's good, D-Boy? I was busy," Dirty Redd said as Sarah wiped saliva from her chin.

"You're lucky that you called me back. An assassin connected with Heron is coming your way, and we think you should vacate the room immediately."

"What you mean?" Dirty Redd immediately became concerned.

Sarah could hear the conversation.

"We know you're with Sarah. Agent J is on his there now."

When Sarah heard those last words, she jumped up. "Let's go! We have to get out of here now!"

D-Boy heard her voice and immediately knew who she was. He still thought she had something to do with Prime's death, but he couldn't prove it. He also thought Dirty Redd was stupid for dealing with her again, knowing she was moving with the opposition.

She practically dragged Dirty Redd toward the door. "You have to leave your stuff here if you want to live. Agent J is a psychopath on steroids."

Those last words got him in gear. "Let me get my Goyard bag. It has $30K in it." He ran to the closet to retrieve his money bag, and they raced out of the suite.

John hacked into the hotel's security cameras and saw Dirty Redd and Sarah walking rapidly down the hallway toward the elevator. He switched to the parking lot and saw Agent J rapidly approaching the hotel entrance.

"Tell them to wait before they get on the elevator. Agent J is in the lobby about to enter the elevator going to the penthouse floor."

D-Boy relayed the message. "What should they do now?" D-Boy asked John.

"Let Agent J get on the elevator first, and then they can get on going down."

Agent J got on the elevator and rode it to the top floor, where the penthouse suite was located. Sarah and Dirty Redd hid in an adjacent hallway corner, waiting for the elevator to open. Only one elevator went to the penthouse suite, so they had to time it perfectly.

The elevator stopped, and Agent J got off and headed toward the suite. Sarah saw him screwing the silencer on his gun as the elevator doors closed. It started its way back down before they could get on it. Sarah quickly ran to the elevator and pressed the button for it to come back up. When it stopped, the doors opened with a ring of a bell, causing Agent J to turn around. That's when he saw Sarah and Dirty Redd rushing to enter the elevator.

Before the door closed, Agent J let off five shots in their direction. They both stood on the side of the closing door while bullets hit the back of the elevator. Finally, the doors closed, and Sarah pressed the button to descend, but the elevator moved slowly as it descended.

Agent J saw a door that read *Stairs*, so he ran down the stairs as quickly as possible. He was moving faster than the elevator so he would be on the first floor before them. He had to run down 20 flights of stairs, but he was physically fit for the task.

As the elevator lowered, it stopped on the tenth floor to

let someone on. Sarah made a frustrated face when a stunning Black woman got on. Sarah's expression wasn't because she had disdain for the woman, but it gave Agent J more time to reach the lobby. The woman rolled her eyes at Sarah. Then she noticed Dirty Redd and changed her demeanor.

"Dirty Redd? I thought that was you. I love your music." The woman was in full fan mode. "Can I take a pic with you?" The elevator stopped on the first floor.

"Not right now. We're in a rush," he quickly replied.

"You don't have to be nasty. All I'm trying to do is show you love," the woman said aggressively.

The elevator doors opened just as Agent J opened the stairwell door and entered the lobby. His timing was impeccable because the angry fan was talking to them when Sarah saw Agent J.

She immediately pushed the woman out of the way.

"Bitch! Who are you pushing?"

Her last words were cut off by the sound of bullets hitting the back of the elevator wall, missing her by inches. Sarah crouched and started duckwalking. Dirty Redd did the same. They had cover from the chairs and people in the lobby. She picked up a fire extinguisher and sprayed the white powdery substance directly at Agent J, causing him to choke and cover his eyes. It created a smoke screen that they used to reach the side exit.

"This way!" Sarah instructed.

They reached the Corvette and escaped. Agent J was forced to go to a water fountain to rinse his eyes and face. He looked at his phone's GPS, which was tracking Sarah's car, but it wasn't moving.

They took another vehicle, he quickly surmised. "They got away," he reported to Heron.

"What the fuck you mean they got away?" Heron yelled.

"Someone tipped them off because they were ready when I got there. There was no way for them to know I was coming for them."

Heron thought, *It had to be the lawyer John.*

Agent J agreed because he knew more about John than he let on. He knew precisely who he was. He was a mystery to everyone but Agent J, but he didn't want to trip the wire by letting Heron know too much. It would blow his cover.

"John, the lawyer?" Agent J pretended not to know who he was talking about.

"Yeah, he's the mastermind behind this whole fucking mess. If it weren't for him, D-Boy would've never discovered the operation."

"I can't even follow them because they switched cars." Agent J was fuming because they made a fool of him.

"Just come back to the safe house." Heron ended the call and made a new one. "That was real cute, D-Boy!"

"What're you talking about?"

"You can play stupid all you want, but the only person who'll suffer is your grandfather."

"Hold on, he has nothing to do with this," D-Boy responded angrily.

"You should've thought about that before you decided to warn Sarah."

D-Boy was about to panic, but he knew he had an ace in his hand. "Listen, I have a proposal for you. I have the secret formula for the Diaz brothers' Nitro. Once I give it to you, you can grow it yourself and cut them out, making you the sole seller of Nitro."

"Let me guess. You'll give me the formula in exchange for your grandfather."

"Exactly." D-Boy paused to let him think it over.

Just like John and D-Boy predicted, Heron took the bait hook, line, and sinker. He couldn't resist the power grab. He knew having the formula for Nitro would bring him closer to his goal of being a billionaire. He was obsessed with having power to the point where it blinded him. There was no turning back for Heron. He was absolutely corrupt to his core.

"You have 24 hours to bring me the formula, or your grandfather is dead." Heron hung up.

"You heard what he said, John. How close are you to cracking the code?" D-Boy asked.

"Close, but no cigar. It could take me about two days the way it's looking." John knew it wasn't the answer he was looking for.

"What are we going to do? He said he would kill Grandpa Joe if I didn't have the formula in 24 hours."

"All I can do is work overtime on cracking the code. In the meantime, you need to keep your composure around the Diaz brothers. The incident in the garage could blow your cover. I was able to loop the footage by the garage, but I can't stop them from snooping. Be careful."

Rodolfo stood outside D-Boy's room door, trying to listen to his conversation. When D-Boy opened the door, he bumped into him. "Pardon me."

"You're good." Rodolfo gave D-Boy an inquiring look before walking to Fernando's office.

You must have been standing at my door for me to bump into you like that, D-Boy thought—*no time for that. I need to see Grandpa Joe.* He walked to the garage and drove off in the Rolls-Royce.

Rodolfo and Fernando watched D-Boy on the monitor. "I can't put my finger on it, but there's something about him that isn't adding up," Rodolfo said.

"What do you mean?" Fernando asked.

"I didn't see him take anything at the storage, but when I tried to do a thorough background check on him, it was like he's a ghost."

Fernando scratched his chin. "Explain."

"His history stops at 25 years old. From there, it's like there's no activity. It goes blank. The only people that I see follow that pattern are undercover agents. I'm not saying he is one. It's just a red flag."

Fernando thought out loud. "He is like a fucking ghost. That's how Haitian John acted when he saw him. He even said D-Boy was somebody from his past that he thought was either dead or dealt with. Then he popped up in place of Haitian John to be the liaison for whoever was shipping tons of Nitro for me. That's why D-Boy is important to my organization. Without him, I can't ship tons of Nitro into the United States because I don't know who is behind the scenes."

"I understand. I'll keep a close eye on him." Rodolfo walked out of the office and went straight to his room.

In his closet was an array of spy equipment, everything from microcameras the size of a penny to listening and tracking devices. He had spy drones and an arsenal of weapons from grenades, rocket launchers, and flamethrowers. He was ready for war. One thing he learned as King Cobra's second in command was always to expect the worst. Then you'll never be caught off guard.

He took out three listening devices and two microcameras, then walked to D-Boy's room. The door was locked, but Rodolfo had a specially designed skeleton key to open any door lock. Once inside, he strategically placed the devices around the room. When he finished, he locked the door and went to his room to test the efficiency of the cameras.

"Perfect. Now let's see who you *really* are." Smiling, he sat back, watched the screen, and waited.

THE SAFE HOUSE

D-Boy pulled into the driveway of the safe house. He was greeted by Agent J at the door, who gave him the same hateful look as always. D-Boy knew Agent J couldn't wait to kill his grandfather slowly, so he gave him the same hateful stare. D-Boy wasn't scared of Agent J. He might not have the same training as him, but he had heart. You can't be taught that. You had to be born with it; it had to be in your DNA.

He walked past Agent J without saying a word, then went straight to Heron's office and entered without knocking. Heron was sitting in his chair smoking a cigar. "My favorite nigger on the planet. D-Boy." He blew out smoke as he spoke.

"I want to see my grandfather."

"I don't know about that since you and John pulled that little stunt with Sarah and Dirty Redd. He's off-limits until you give me the formula." He smiled before taking a pull of the cigar, this time, disrespectfully blowing the smoke in D-Boy's face.

D-Boy waved his hand in the air to fan away the smoke from him. "You dirty motherfucker."

"The dirty motherfucker is your friend Dirty Redd. If it wasn't for him, you wouldn't be in this mess. You should've warned him not to get involved. Now, you have to pay the consequences." He blew more smoke in D-Boy's face and looked at his watch, "You got like 18 hours before I blow Grandpa Joe's head off. Now, go get me the formula."

Agent J entered the office and was standing behind D-Boy with a menacing look on his face. "Just give me the word, and I'll clean him up and his grandfather."

D-Boy turned around and pushed Agent J. "Back up off me! You ain't cleaning up nobody."

Before Agent J could retaliate, Heron shouted, "Agent J, stand down!"

Agent J had his fist balled up, ready to strike, but he took a deep breath and stormed out of the office.

Heron looked at his watch again. "Time is ticking." He tapped the face of his watch. "Go get me that formula."

D-Boy left the office and drove off, trying to keep his composure. He knew it was out of his control now. Heron had the upper hand. All he could do now was count on John to figure out the formula.

He drove the Rolls-Royce as fast as he thought. His silence was interrupted by the sound of John's voice in his ear. "Slow down before you kill yourself. Control your emotions like I taught you. Now, take a deep breath and concentrate on the mission."

John's words were hypnotic because D-Boy snapped into a trance and began to breathe as John instructed. With each breath, he redirected his negative thoughts. After the tenth breath, the car was traveling at a moderate speed of 80 mph from the 160 mph he was previously driving at. He was instantly back to being focused on the mission.

"That's my boy. Now, relax and let me decode this drug. I got this. I'm closer to figuring it out than I thought. I'll keep you posted." John ended the conversation.

D-Boy made it to the Diaz mansion in record time. When he reached his room, he lay down and turned on the television. He scrolled through the channels, searching for something interesting to watch. That's when he saw her. It was Dalia. Some guy was interviewing her that D-Boy didn't recognize.

"The people want to know more about you, like what your love life looks like. Is there a Prince Charming for the Princess of Marrakesh?" the guy asked, obviously flirting with her.

"Yes, there's a Prince Charming, but he's back in the United States." She gave her signature infectious smile, which caused D-Boy to smile.

"That's my baby." He immediately called her. "Hey, baby, I was just watching your interview with some cheesy dude."

She laughed. "He was cheesy and kept trying to flirt with me."

"I bet a lot of men are flirting with you since you are the princess of Marrakesh."

"None of that means anything if I don't have you."

"We have a plan to free my grandfather. This will all be over soon, and then I can fly to Marrakesh to be with you." He couldn't contain his feelings for Dalia. It was the first time he felt this way about a woman in a long time.

"I would love that."

"Princess Dalia, it's time to meet with your counsel." The voice of her aide interrupted their conversation.

"OK, give me a second." Her aide departed. "D-Boy, I have to go. Can I call you back later this afternoon?"

"Yeah, but remember, your afternoon is like my 4:00 a.m. But you can call anytime, and I'll answer."

"OK, baby, I love you." She hung up.

D-Boy couldn't stop smiling as he lay in the comfortable bed thinking about Dalia. He drifted off to sleep in a matter of minutes with his thoughts. The hidden camera and listening devices caught the entire conversation.

"That was interesting," Rodolfo said as he watched D-Boy resting. "The princess of Marrakesh. And what was he talking about when he's finished here?" Rodolfo rewound the conversation.

"We have a plan to free my grandfather. This will all be over soon, and then I can fly to Marrakesh to be with you."

"The plan to free his grandfather . . . It sounds like he's being forced to be the middleman for whoever is shipping the Nitro." He played it back two more times. "This will all be over soon. What will all be over soon? That's the million-dollar question."

Rodolfo stayed up all night trying to decipher the message so he could report to his new boss. He was trying to prove himself worthy before they decided to kill him for proving the opposite. He knew the game he was playing because he had played it his whole life: the role of second fiddle.

His ultimate goal was to be the boss of this operation. He didn't care about Captain Diaz; he said that to spare his life. He would kill Captain Diaz, King Cobra, and the Diaz brothers to be the number one. He was tired of living under the thumb of a number one.

"Soon, I'll be the king." He took a healthy swig from a bottle of tequila before heading to the office to inform Fernando about his discovery of the infamous D-Boy.

CHAPTER 14
THE WARLORD

JOHN SAT in the Warlord's laboratory section, working overtime to unravel the secret ingredients of Nitro. He was able to separate everything so he could examine what the secret component was.

"So far, I see the basic components of the coca plant, but there is something there that I need to break down."

He was finally able to isolate the one thing that was foreign. "It appears to be some kind of acid, like a psychedelic of some kind."

He looked up the components of all the psychedelic drugs on the market and noticed one thing: they all had to be fermented in cow dung. "That was how mushrooms were made from the acid in the cows' feces."

As he examined further, he saw that it wasn't cow dung. "If it's not the cows' shit, it's some kind of acid that creates a similar psychedelic effect mixed with the adrenaline rush from the coca plant."

John was getting tired, but there was no time for sleep.

He racked his brain, trying to figure out what the secret ingredient could be. He liked to fast when he was in scientist mode because it allowed him to focus more. It also caused him to urinate a lot. He stepped outside of the Warlord, pulled out his penis, and began to urinate on a tree. The stream hitting the tree created a fog from the mixture of cool air and the warm stream of his urine.

That's when it hit him. "It's not the cow's shit. It's the cow's urine." He pissed on his hand from moving too fast to get back to the lab to test out his new theory.

Again, he looked at the isolated element, only this time, he asked his computer to analyze it as cow urine. Thirty seconds later, the computer came up with a perfect match for the added component to Nitro.

"I'll be a monkey's uncle! The secret formula to Nitro's super potency is fucking cow piss." He immediately called D-Boy. "I cracked the code, and you won't believe this."

"At this point, I'll believe anything. Lay it on me." D-Boy was mentally exhausted from all this drama.

"The secret ingredient to the Diaz brothers' formula is fucking cow urine. They fertilize their crops with cow piss, which is a form of psychedelic because of the high concentration of acid.

"In layman's terms, these cats are making billions because they added cow piss to their cocaine crops."

D-Boy started laughing uncontrollably. "You mean to tell me *that's* the secret to all this shit? These dudes are unbelievable."

"I have to say, they're fucking geniuses." John laughed along with D-Boy.

D-Boy looked at his watch. "We got two hours, so let's get to the safe house to save Grandpa Joe."

Suddenly, a warning popped up on John's screen. It informed him of the detected surveillance equipment. "Oh fuck, someone is listening. We've been compromised!" John pulled up the schematics of the Diaz mansion, and it showed hidden cameras and listening devices in D-Boy's room. "Don't say another word. There are hidden cameras and listening devices in your room. Rodolfo is in his room listening to us as we speak. You need to isolate him ASAP before he alerts the Diaz brothers."

D-Boy stepped out of the room, quickly walking toward Rodolfo's room out of earshot of the bugs in his room. "When you say, 'isolate him,' you mean fuck him up or take him out?"

"There's no need for you to kill him. He just needs to be unconscious for about an hour. So yeah, fuck him up."

"My pleasure. I never liked this motherfucker anyway."

Rodolfo knew D-Boy was coming his way because of the cameras. He didn't realize that D-Boy was on to him spying on him. Now, Rodolfo was in a bad position because he assumed that the element of surprise was his when, in fact, he was the one about to be caught off guard.

D-Boy knocked on his door. "It's D-Boy. I need to ask you a question."

"Come in." Rodolfo was sitting in a chair when D-Boy entered.

"I wanted to know—" In midsentence, D-Boy swiftly wrapped his arms around Rodolfo's neck and applied enough pressure to put him to sleep in seconds. Then he looked at the footage Rodolfo was watching and deleted it. Finished, he rushed past Fernando's office toward the garage to grab a car. Fernando noticed D-Boy running past his office, so he followed him. When he got to the garage, Fernando called out.

"Yo, D-Boy!"

D-Boy was startled. "What's up, Fernando?"

"Everything OK? I saw you running to the garage." Fernando was suspicious.

"Oh yeah. I have to go see my grandfather in the hospital before 9:00, so I was in a rush; that's all. Everything good with you?"

Fernando looked at D-Boy with apprehension. "I need to talk to you when you get back."

"OK, I'll see you when I return."

I'm not returning; this is it for me, D-Boy thought.

He jumped into the Rolls-Royce and left the mansion. After John cracked the code on Nitro and they gave it to Heron, there was no need to deal with the Diaz brothers anymore. D-Boy despised the drug game and everything that came with it. He didn't care how much money drugs made; it destroyed lives. The Karma that came with it was real.

When he got to the safe house, John sat in the Warlord waiting for him. "You ready to get this over with?" John asked.

"Of course. I've put this drug shit behind me, and after this, I'll be moving to Marrakesh with my princess," D-Boy responded.

"Sounds like a plan."

Heron's voice spoke over a speaker by the gate. "Let's

get this over with." The gate opened, and they drove through it.

Agent J met them at the door with his signature scowl. D-Boy wanted to fight him so badly, but he knew there was no time for that now. Grandpa Joe was waiting for them in the foyer instead of his room.

D-Boy hugged him. "You OK, Grandpa?"

"I'm OK. It was a walk in the park." Grandpa Joe was tougher than he looked.

"Hand over the formula," Heron commanded.

John handed him a piece of paper, and Heron started reading it. "This says that the secret ingredient is just some cow piss?" Agent J laughed when Heron read the formula.

"That's it. Cow piss acts as a psychedelic when sprayed on cocaine crops. That's why Nitro has the effect that it does," John explained.

"It doesn't matter; we gave you the formula, now let us go." D-Boy was ready to leave.

"Not so fast." Agent J pulled out a gun on them. "You didn't think I was going to let you just walk out of here, did you?"

"You gave your word," D-Boy said to Heron.

"I had my fingers crossed."

Agent J hit D-Boy in the back of his head with the butt of his gun, and he fell to the floor. "That's for the other day."

"Take them to the cell," Heron ordered.

John secretly pressed a button on his key chain that unleashed his robot soldiers. The Warlord had four compartments that opened up by the wheel well. Two dog robots and two human-size robots were deployed.

"What are we going to do?" D-Boy asked John.

"Five, four, three, two, one." When John said "one," the front door was hit by an explosive that blew it off its hinges.

The two robotic dogs raced in while shooting .40-caliber bullets from a barrel in their mouths. The two human robots came in behind the dogs. One was shooting, and the other one threw fire from a built-in flamethrower.

Agent J shot at the robots, but they were bulletproof. Heron took refuge in his office, leaving Agent J to fend for himself. One of the bullets hit Agent J in his shoulder, causing him to fall back. The flamethrower lit the foyer on fire, and it spread fast.

Heron had an emergency escape hatch in his office. There was a bobsled that went straight down, then shot straight ahead until it hit the exit hatch half a mile away. He struggled to open it while one of the robots used the flamethrower against the door, but the door was bomb- and fireproof.

The other robot picked the lock to the cell the three men were in. Once it was open, all three ran out but couldn't get past the fire by the door. The other robot sprayed fire retardant on the flames by the front door, putting it out enough for them to run through it.

As they exited, Agent J grabbed D-Boy. "Where do you think you're going?" He struck him, knocking D-Boy unconscious.

John and Grandpa Joe didn't notice that D-Boy wasn't with them until they reached the Warlord. "Where's D-Boy?" Grandpa Joe asked.

They looked back at the house, which was going up in flames. "He must be in the house," John replied.

"We have to go back in there and get him!" Grandpa Joe shouted.

"We can't. The fire is too big. We won't make it!" John was forcing Grandpa Joe into the truck.

"NO!" Grandpa Joe struggled to free himself from John's grip, but to no avail. John easily overpowered the older man and threw him inside the truck.

Agent J took out a knife and was ready to torture D-Boy when he got up. "You ain't taking me out that easy." D-Boy hit him so hard that he fell into the flames, burning his back and causing him to move forward toward D-Boy. That's when D-Boy kicked Agent J in his chest, causing his whole body to fall into the flames. He instantly caught fire and tried frantically running to put out the flames.

D-Boy got up, ran through the front door, and made it to the Warlord. "Wait for me!" he yelled, knocking on the window.

"D-Boy!" Grandpa Joe yelled.

"I knew you would make it. What happened to Agent J and Heron?" John asked.

"Heron locked himself in his office, and Agent J caught on fire and was running through the house trying to put himself out. I think he's dead."

"Let's get out of here." John pressed a button, and the robots recoiled into their hidden compartment by the wheel well.

The fire department entered the gate as they drove away from the scene. When they arrived, they quickly put out the fire. Upon further inspection, one of the firefighters saw

Agent J sprawled out on the back lawn by the pool. He was severely burnt and unconscious.

"Hey, we got a survivor over here." The firefighter checked his pulse. It was faint, but he was alive.

"Let's get him to the hospital ASAP!"

They put him on a stretcher, then into the ambulance, where they gave him oxygen to revive his smoke-filled lungs. His vital signs were still weak, but he was hanging in there. Agent J was alive.

"This guy is very strong. He has burns on 90 percent of his body, and his lungs had so much smoke in them it's a miracle that he's still breathing."

"Were there any other survivors?" the fire chief asked.

"None we can see. It looks like everyone got out besides that guy." He pointed toward Agent J.

"OK, guys, let's shut this down so we can leave."

THE BOBSLED STOPPED ABRUPTLY, causing Heron to take a deep breath. He had a few cuts and bruises, but other than that, he was OK. He stood up and brushed himself off before taking out his phone and calling Director Cohen on a video call.

"You look like shit," Cohen said while smiling. "What the fuck happened to you?"

"D-Boy. That's what happened to me."

"Well, that's it. Special Agent Heron, this operation is officially over. I mean it. If I hear you still carrying out this operation, I'll have you court-martialed for treason and executed by a firing squad. Do you understand me?"

"Yes, sir, Director Cohen."

"Good, now get your ass back to Langley. I have a recruit I need you to train." Cohen hung up.

Heron looked at his phone. He had 1 percent left on his battery. "Fuck." He started walking in the direction of the bright lights up ahead. "It's not over, D-Boy."

THE DIAZ MANSION

Rodolfo woke up rubbing his head. "What happened?" He tried to recall how he ended up on the floor with a headache. He took a deep breath, searching his mind.

"I was watching D-Boy in his room, and he said something that was suspect. What was it?" He couldn't remember what he was listening to D-Boy say. "He said something about cracking the code or something like that. I can't fucking remember."

He looked at the monitor and rewound the footage to see if any of it would jog his memory. He saw D-Boy lying on the bed talking to Dalia, but nothing was out of the ordinary. Then it came back to him—how D-Boy put him in a headlock.

"That motherfucker put me to sleep." It all came back to him now. "He was telling someone to get the formula for Nitro." He ran to Fernando's office. "D-Boy is trying to find the formula to Nitro!"

"What you mean?" Fernando said while eating a bowl of fruit.

"I caught him on camera making some deal or something about learning the secret ingredient."

"Where is D-Boy? He didn't come back from the hospital yet?" Fernando took his phone and pressed an app that would find his Rolls-Royce. "It says the car is at this location, but this isn't no hospital." Fernando became suspicious, so he called D-Boy. "D-Boy, what's going on? I'm hearing some shady stuff about you. I hope it isn't true."

Diego joined them in the office. "What's going on?"

Fernando put up his finger for him to be silent and listen. "Where are you?"

"It doesn't matter. All you need to know is that it's over. I'm done being the middleman for the CIA. Yes, you heard me right. They're the people that you're doing business with. They have been shipping tons of your precious Nitro into the United States. But don't worry. As long as you're making that money, you'll be OK."

"What about you? What are you going to do?" Fernando asked.

"Good question. All I know is that I'm done with the drug game once and for all. You can have it. Good luck, Fernando." D-Boy hung up.

John drove the Warlord toward New York. He was dead tired from all the excitement and stress. He put the Warlord on autopilot and fell asleep. D-Boy and Grandpa Joe were in the back relaxing. They too had a lot of excitement today, especially Grandpa Joe.

"Man, that Agent J was a piece of work," Grandpa Joe said.

D-Boy shook his head. "He almost killed me with one punch. I've never been hit that hard in my life."

"Is he alive?"

"I don't know. I hope so. He was on fire running through the house when I escaped."

"What you think about those fucking robots? If it wasn't for them, we'd be dead." Grandpa Joe was animated when he spoke.

"I know. That was a surprise. I'm thankful we had them because I thought it was over. I should've known John had something up his sleeve."

"It's good to have you back, D-Boy."

"It's good to be back, Grandpa Joe." He put his arm around him and held his grandfather close for the whole ride to New York.

CHAPTER 15
THE ROYAL PALACE AT MARRAKESH, MORROCCO
TWO YEARS LATER . . .

D-Boy stepped out on the balcony, looking at the beautiful landscape of the palace grounds. Dalia came up and hugged him from behind. D-Boy turned around, and they locked eyes and kissed, but little hands pulled on Dalia's dress, interrupting the lovers' embrace.

"Look, Mommy, I found a lizard." The little tyke held a lizard in his hand.

"Boy, you better get that lizard away from me!" Dalia was afraid of lizards.

D-Boy laughed. "DJ, you know your mother is scared of those lizards."

"I'm not," he said defiantly. "I'm like you, right, Daddy?"

"That's right, my little brave man." D-Boy picked him up and kissed him on the cheek.

Dalia let out a sigh of pain. "This baby is kicking my ass. She kicks me every time she hears her brother's voice."

D-Boy rubbed her stomach. "Good thing you only got a

couple weeks until she is ready to grace the world with her beautiful presence, just like her mother." D-Boy kissed her forehead.

"I wish my mother would've lived to see her grandchildren. She would spoil them to death." Dalia shed a tear. "I miss her so much."

"I know, baby. Look at it this way . . . She's here in spirit watching over us. I don't believe in death. I believe she's here, just not in the physical realm."

"You always say the right things. That's why I love you."

They were interrupted by a knock on the door. "Excuse me, Queen Dalia. It's time for your daily briefing."

"I will be there in a few," Dalia responded.

The royal couple dressed in the traditional Marrakesh garments before heading to the Royal Hall. Daily, Dalia had to be briefed on matters of the kingdom. It was time-consuming, but she loved her role.

"Introducing King Darius and Queen Dalia." They were announced the same way every single day.

"I can get used to this king life," D-Boy said with a smile.

Dalia grabbed his hand. "I can get used to you being a king too, my King."

D-Boy smiled and looked at Darius Junior. "What about you, DJ? You like this king life?"

"I'm the prince, Daddy." DJ smiled at his father.

"That's right. You're a prince."

Queen Dalia went through the daily ritual of being briefed on the empire's business. She sat on the royal throne at eight-and-a-half months pregnant. She was glowing so much everyone could actually see it.

"That will be all for today," Dalia's assistant said.

Dalia moved to rise from the throne, and water suddenly fell to the ground from under her dress. She closed her eyes and looked at D-Boy.

"It's that time," she said, knowing that her little princess was ready to join the family.

"Let's go, DJ. You ready to be a big brother?"

"I'm ready, Daddy!"

D-Boy looked at his beautiful wife and son and smiled. All he could do was smile.

THE END

???

ALSO BY BILLIGOAT

ABOUT THE AUTHOR

When you think of a 'Renaissance Man', Alah Adams fits the description perfectly! He's authored 7 novels and ghost-written 4 books for iconic names in hip hop—Rakim Allah, Erick Sermon of EPMD, super-producer Drumma Boy, and Mama Jones. In 2020, he launched the Billigoat clothing line with the motto: "You don't need a billion dollars to have a billionaire mindset." Now, he's bringing his vision to the screen with a film series based on his *American D-Boy* trilogy.